Just Add Friendship

AN
Everly Falls
NOVEL

Just Add Friendship

HEATHER B. MOORE

Copyright © 2023 by Heather B. Moore
Paperback edition
All rights reserved.

No part of this book may be reproduced in any form whatsoever without prior written permission of the publisher, except in the case of brief passages embodied in critical reviews and articles. This is a work of fiction. The characters, names, incidents, places, and dialogue are products of the author's imagination and are not to be construed as real.
Interior design by Cora Johnson
Edited by JL Editing Services and Lorie Humpherys
Cover design by Rachael Anderson
Cover image credit: Deposit Photos #467469484
Published by Mirror Press, LLC
ISBN: 978-1-952611-38-4

EVERLY FALLS SERIES:
Just Add Romance
Just Add Mischief
Just Add Friendship

PINE VALLEY SERIES:
Worth the Risk
Where I Belong
Say You Love Me
Waiting for You
Finding Us
Until We Kissed
Let's Begin Again
All For You

PROSPERITY RANCH SERIES:
One Summer Day
Steal My Heart
Not Over You
Seasoned with Love
Take a Chance

HISTORICAL TITLES:
The Paper Daughters of Chinatown
The Slow March of Light
In the Shadow of a Queen
Under the Java Moon
Until Vienna
Love is Come
Esther the Queen
Ruth
The Moses Chronicles
Mary and Martha
Hannah
Rebekah and Isaac

Just Add Friendship

Ten years of dating since he left. Ten years of nothing working out. Is it her, or is it him? Or can no one else measure up?

Stephenie Grady can't figure out why every man she dates turns into a troll. Well, not an actual troll with green skin and warts, or the kind of troll who stalks the internet with negative comments, but the kind of troll who dumps her. Yes, she's been dumped every time, by every guy she's dated. She'd blame it on the male population, but her girlfriends have amazing men in their lives.

Steph could also tell herself she hasn't met the right man yet, and that could be true, but what if she already has? What if the right man was in her life ten years ago, and what if he comes to their ten-year high school reunion? And what if her memories of a past relationship don't measure up to the realities of the boy-turned-man, Cal Conner?

One

BRANDY, ARE YOU BRINGING IAN? Stephenie Grady texted her group chat of high school friends on her short break at the salon. Well, the ladies were her *former* high school friends. It had been ten years now. After they'd all split up and gone to college or followed other pursuits, somehow they'd ended up back in Everly Falls. Best friends once again.

Yeah, he's coming. Brandy added a heart emoji. She and her older sister Everly were both in the group text. *Are you bringing a date?*

That was the question of the day, or maybe of the year. Steph dated a lot. But nothing long term, and therein lay the problem. She didn't have a special someone to bring to her ten-year high school reunion. And in a small town like Everly Falls, showing up without a date would scream one thing: I Don't Have My Life Together.

Well, that might be a tad dramatic, but it was how Steph felt some of the time. Okay, most of the time. Especially when her closest friends were either married, married with kids, engaged, or about to be engaged. Lori was the exception, but she was sort of a closed-off person and didn't really seem to care about having a plus-one at social events. Besides, she'd be out of town for the reunion.

A customer came into the salon, but from where Steph sat toward the back, she could see it wasn't anyone for her. So she returned to her texting.

Haven't decided yet, Steph texted the group. *If Lori were coming, I'd just go with her.*

Sorry, again, Lori wrote. *The committee should have checked my schedule first.* Winking face emoji.

Steph sent a crying emoji because she was in fact on said committee. Which made it even more awkward to show up without a date. Everyone on the committee was buzzing about what they were going to wear and what their spouse/significant other would be wearing.

Maybe she could catch a sudden illness. Was the flu going around yet? It was September . . . No, even as she thought it, she knew she'd suffer from a severe case of FOMO—fear of missing out. It was her crutch in life. She supposed staying off social media would help, but that would be like a bee abandoning its hive.

Speaking of bees . . .

He had called her Bee.

A nickname that led to their one and only date, because she'd tutored him in English class. He'd told her she was freakishly good at spelling, and she'd confessed that until junior high, she'd entered all the spelling bees and won.

He might be at the high school reunion. *Might* being the operative word because apparently he wasn't on social media. Not anywhere. Yep, she'd checked, and short of hiring a private investigator, she had no idea where he currently lived or worked. So either Cal Conner received the mailed invitation to his last known address, or he didn't. Maybe he'd moved, or he was in jail, or he was dead.

Yes, Steph had considered all options.

Especially the more desirable option of Cal coming to

the reunion—by some miracle only the cosmos knew how to make happen. But what if he brought his supermodel girlfriend, or perhaps even a supermodel wife. Neither would be surprising.

What's going on with Nate? Julie texted the group. She was married, with a toddler and another baby on the way. Her plus-one would be her husband Dave.

Ah, Nate . . . Steph drew in a breath before replying. *Our date the other night ended with a phone call from his ex, which he took while I was in the car. Let's just say I got out and called an Uber to take me home.*

The sympathy texts poured in after that. Steph usually reported on her dates right after they were done, mostly because Julie begged her to—entertainment for the "boring married woman," according to her. But Steph wasn't quite over this incident, so she hadn't shared it right away.

The bell over the door of the shop tinkled as a customer pushed their way inside. It was her next client. She stood and walked through the salon, skirting around the clumps of cut hair on the ground and bypassing the murmuring conversations of the other stylists and their clients.

"Mrs. Kane," Steph said once she reached the front of the shop. "How are you?"

"Call me Lydia, dear." The woman, who was Brandy and Everly's mother, smiled her perfect lipstick smile. Steph didn't know Lydia Kane's age—maybe late fifties? But she was definitely someone Steph aspired to be: a woman impeccably dressed, dolled-up hair, perfect makeup. Today, Lydia wore a colorful plaid scarf with a soft beige sweater, paired with herringbone trousers and suede boots. She looked like she'd stepped out of a fall fashion catalog.

"You're looking beautiful today, Lydia," Steph said with a smile.

"Thank you. You're kind to say so." Her blue gaze swept over Steph. "I love that dress."

"Oh, thank you." She flashed another smile. Dresses were her signature outfit. Once it grew colder, she'd have to pull out the thick tights. Although winters in Everly Falls were more rain than the rare snow.

Lydia sat in the salon chair, and Steph settled a soft black cape over her shoulders.

"What are you thinking today?" she asked as she ran her fingers through the older woman's fine strands.

Lydia's eyes were a darker blue than Brandy's, and her short bob with silver and blonde streaks had grown out a little jagged.

"Oh, more of the same, I think." Lydia smoothed a hand over her neck and tilted her head. "Maybe more of an A-line cut versus the usual blunt bob?"

"I can do that." Steph met Lydia's smile in the mirror. "And the color? Any changes?"

"If you think I'm going completely silver, that'll never happen. Just give me the usual highlights." Lydia's smile turned speculative. "I have a date tonight."

"Wonderful," Steph gushed, while inside her stomach knotted. "Do I know him? Is he local?" Did her daughters know? From all the conversations she had ever overheard, Lydia had sworn off dating. Surely the topic of Lydia going on her first date in a long time would have come up in the group chat. She'd been widowed for many years, and no man could match up to her dearly departed husband.

"You don't know him. He's from the next town over." Lydia grinned like the Cheshire Cat.

"Oh, interesting." Steph gathered the foils and color, then dropped her voice when she returned. "Is this your first date?"

"Yes," Lydia confirmed. "But it feels like I already know him. We've been messaging for weeks."

The phrase sent Steph on alert. "Messaging? You mean texting?" She mixed the color in a small plastic bowl.

Lydia's eyes crinkled with humor. "No, dear. Messaging on a dating app. Isn't that how it's done these days? I hear you date a lot—isn't that how you meet all those men?"

Steph opened her mouth, then closed it. She sectioned off Lydia's hair and started on the first foil. "I, uh . . . I've been on some apps, but not for a while." It had been too hard to filter through the crazies. Her last app date was two years ago, when she showed up at a restaurant, only to be met by a man twice the age he'd claimed on his profile. She hadn't stayed long enough to ask him where he'd dug up the photo he'd posted.

That night she'd deleted the app, and hadn't regretted it for a second. Except now . . . "Which app did you use?" Maybe things had cleaned up in the past couple of years, and there were more filters or something.

"Oh, it's kind of a spunky name." Lydia pulled out her phone from her glossy red purse. "Friends to More. You can set your profile to 'friends only' or 'looking for more.' Spiffy, huh?"

Steph had never heard of the app. She finished up one section of hair, then started on the next. "Sounds interesting." She was pretty sure all dating apps had those features, but she didn't want to deflate Lydia's excitement. "What do your daughters think?"

Lydia laughed. "I'm not telling them—they'd throw a fit. If the gentleman turns out to be everything I hope he is, then I'll let my daughters know."

Steph laughed as well, but her gut had tightened again. There were so many scams going around, and a beautiful—

and somewhat naïve and small-town—woman like Lydia Kane would be the perfect target.

Steph drew in a steadying breath. "I hope your date goes well. I'm excited to hear about it later. Where are you meeting?" She told herself she was only asking out of curiosity, but a small warning bell continued to ring in her head.

"It's a Mexican restaurant in Wintree," Lydia said in a breezy voice. "He said he'd send me the directions later this afternoon."

Steph's smile stiffened. "Do you like Mexican food?"

"For the most part," Lydia said. "I just don't usually eat it for dinner." She lowered her voice. "Heartburn, you know."

Steph nodded and said in a light tone, "I've heard all about heartburn from my grandpa. Say, do you have a picture of your mystery man, and does he have a name?"

"Sure do." Lydia looked about the shop as if she expected someone else to be leaning over to listen to their conversation. Seemingly safe, she opened her photo app and showed a picture of a forty-something man in a plaid shirt, posing next to a fishing boat.

Steph's eyes widened involuntarily. "Oh, he's . . . good looking."

"He sure is." Lydia released a swoony sigh. "And I know what you're thinking—he's too young for me. But he said he's looking for a mature woman. Not too mature, of course. Oh, and his name is Greg. Kind of catchy." She laughed.

Steph memorized as much as she could about the man's features. Dirty-blond hair, mustache, looked just under six feet, bit of a paunch. Maybe it was fine. Maybe he was fine. But she didn't want to take any chances.

After Lydia's appointment, Steph took a deep breath

and texted both Brandy and Everly. *Probably nothing, but your mom came into the salon today. She said she's going on a date tonight—and apparently it's a secret! She met the man on a dating app, so of course I'm a little suspicious. I didn't know your mom was dating, and well . . . I didn't want to betray her confidence, but I thought I should give you gals a heads-up.*

Everly's reply was immediate. *I'm out of town at Austin's parents', so I'm kind of stuck here. Do you think I should call Mom?*

Which dating app? Brandy wrote back at the same time.

Steph typed the name of the app, and within a few minutes, she and Brandy had set up a reconnaissance mission. They'd follow her mom's car to the restaurant and wait outside. It was the least they could do, and it would hopefully ease the worry that kept gnawing at Steph.

Two

"CAN YOU STILL SEE HER?" Brandy asked over the phone.

Steph stood inside a drugstore across the street from the Mexican restaurant Lydia had walked into about five minutes before.

Brandy had parked about a block from the restaurant, and she was now heading to the drugstore as well.

"Not anymore," Steph replied. "She was talking to the hostess. I'm assuming she's sitting down in the lobby waiting for Mystery Guy Named Greg."

"Okay. I hope to get to you before he shows up. Don't want any run-ins with my mom's date."

Steph scoffed. "Right. Especially since you're her mini-me."

"Yeah..." Brandy sighed. "See you in a few."

Steph pocketed her phone and pretended to look at a greeting card rack while keeping an eye on the sidewalk across the street. Maybe she'd overreacted, maybe they all had, but better safe than sorry, right?

The drugstore door opened, and in waltzed Brandy. She was several inches shorter than Steph, making her petite and almost wispy looking. Currently, her shoulder-length blonde hair was covered by a floral scarf, and she wore huge sunglasses. Her signature pearls would give her away to anyone from Everly Falls, especially her mother.

"That's quite . . . obvious." Steph arched her brows. "Undercover?"

Brandy's lips pursed. "Something like that." She joined Steph at the card rack and looked toward the window. "Seen him yet?"

"We literally hung up like fifteen seconds ago." A motion caught her attention, and she grasped Brandy's arm.

"Is that him?" Brandy asked.

Both women looked toward the man who'd come around the corner. He wore a button-down, khaki pants, loafers . . .

"It's definitely him," Steph said, even though she'd only seen his picture for a handful of seconds earlier that day. "Same mustache. Same paunch."

Brandy puffed out a breath of air. "I don't like the way he walks."

Steph arched her brows. "What's wrong with it?" As far as she could tell, he walked normally.

They watched in rapt silence as he slowed in front of the restaurant, checked the watch on his wrist, then pulled open the door and disappeared inside.

"He has a watch," Brandy mused. "Old-fashioned, or creepy?"

"A lot of men wear watches still," Steph said, not sure why she was defending a total stranger whom she was currently stalking.

"Yeah, but he's too young and too old," Brandy said. "Older men wear them because they aren't tied to their cell phones. Younger men wear them to show off that they're wanna-be scuba divers. But men in their forties? It's weird."

"Hmm," Steph mused. "Maybe you're right."

A couple heartbeats passed.

"Hungry?" Brandy asked.

"Don't even think it," she said. "There's no way we can go in there and have your mom not notice us."

Brandy adjusted her giant sunglasses. "She'll be so caught up in her date, she won't be paying attention to the two women wearing scarves in the corner booth." She pulled out a scarf from her small beaded purse.

How it fit inside, Steph wasn't sure. "I'm not wearing this." But she took it anyway and shook it out. "My red hair will be like a flashing beacon no matter how much I can get covered up."

"Either you come, or you don't," Brandy said, handing over the keys, too. "Sit in the car and wait, or try the chicken enchiladas with me."

Steph stared into her friend's lake-blue eyes. There were times when Brandy could be a pushover, but this wasn't one of them. "What's our excuse? Your mom told me about a Mexican restaurant in Wintree, which we both know only has one Mexican restaurant."

Brandy pretended to think. "I dragged you here on short notice because Ian was busy—and I had a coupon to use."

Steph sighed. "You do like couponing."

"I do." Brandy linked their arms and steered her toward the door. "That's our backup explanation, but I'm betting we don't get caught."

"Ten bucks?"

"Pfft. That's high school. It's twenty now."

Steph laughed, and they headed outside into the crisp fall evening.

As they crossed the street after a passing car, Brandy asked, "Are you really going solo to the reunion? Want me to recruit someone?"

Just Add Friendship

"Please, no." Steph squinted over at her as the setting sun blinded her for a moment. "I mean, who is there to set me up with? I know all the available guys in Everly Falls. You and your sister snagged the only new ones."

"There's a few move-ins, and a couple are in Ian's friend group from the gym," Brandy said in a casual tone. "One might be interested."

Steph pulled her to a stop on the sidewalk at the corner of the restaurant. "Don't tell me you've talked about me to someone." She scrunched her nose. "I really don't want to be set up. Just because you're practically engaged to Mr. Hot and Perfect doesn't mean I'm worried about being single for the rest of my life."

Brandy and Ian were definitely close to getting engaged, but Steph suspected they were waiting until after Everly and Austin married in a few weeks, so the spotlight would stay on that magical couple.

Brandy squeezed Steph's arm. "I didn't mean that you need help—you don't need help. It's the *men* who need help." She released her arm and continued to the restaurant doors.

Steph hurried after her. In for a penny, in for a pound.

It was quite amusing to watch Brandy bring on the bossiness and insist the hostess give them a corner booth that was mostly out of sight from the table Lydia and her date were at.

Steph literally held her breath as they followed the hostess to their orange vinyl booth. They settled in and ordered drinks once the server arrived.

"I can't believe we made it," Steph whispered, taking a surreptitious glance over at Lydia. She was telling some story that included a lot of hand gestures. The man laughed. It was a higher-pitched laugh, but not terrible.

"She's flirting," Brandy deadpanned. "It's so . . . weird. He's gotta be at least ten years younger."

"Is the age difference really a big deal?" Steph mused in a hushed voice. "I mean, your mom is a catch for any man."

"My mom *is* a catch. I don't know if he is." Brandy took a sip from her ice water with two lemons. "It's not just that my mother is dating—flirting. She didn't tell me or my sister. And her choice will affect us . . . a lot. Because if things progress and my mother gets married again, I'd have a stepdad."

"Oh yeah, true." Steph took another glance at Lydia and her date. Steph's own mother had a stepdad, Pops, and their personalities clashed. "It would be weird for that guy to be your stepdad."

"Agreed."

Lydia laughed at something her date said. A high, tinkling laugh. Definitely flirting.

Brandy grimaced.

"Maybe he's harmless?" Steph said hopefully. "I mean, should we trust your mom's instincts?"

"Maybe he is harmless, but if she doesn't confess she's gone on a date after this, I'm not going to be happy." Brandy paused. "And we need to make sure he doesn't follow her home."

"What if she invites him?"

Brandy didn't look pleased at the possibility. "I hate this."

Steph reached over and squeezed her hand. "At least we're here. Probably being overprotective, but nothing's going to happen on our watch, okay?"

Brandy exhaled. "Okay."

Their chicken enchiladas came, and Brandy asked the server, "Can you bring to-go containers and the check? We might have to leave pretty soon."

The server bustled away, and Steph took a couple of bites of the cheesy goodness, then noticed Brandy wasn't eating. "Not hungry after all?"

"I'll take it all home," she said. "I can't eat while I'm busy analyzing my mom and her date."

Steph nodded and took another bite. She didn't love heated-up leftovers, but her grandpa loved anything, and since she lived with him, it would be easy to talk him into eating the food.

Soon after the server brought the to-go containers and Brandy had settled the check—she insisted—Lydia and her date stood. They were apparently finished with their meals.

Both Steph and Brandy turned their heads away from the departing couple as they walked toward the front doors.

Once they exited, it was clear they were going to walk together someplace. To their cars? To another shop? Would Lydia get into the man's car?

"Let's go," Brandy said, scooping her meal into the to-go container.

Steph did the same with her meal, and within a handful of moments, they were out the door.

Brandy slowed her step as she looked left, then right. "Where did they go?"

Steph frowned. "Maybe they're browsing one of the shops? Could they have walked fast enough and be at the parking lot already?"

"Let's find out." Brandy headed toward the parking lot behind the restaurant.

"Wait," Steph said. "She might see you . . . I should go."

Brandy hesitated, then nodded. "All right. But get on the phone with me. I'm heading to pick up our car."

Steph hurried toward the back parking lot. She paused before entering into full view, and saw Lydia and her date embracing. At least the hug was brief, then Lydia climbed into her car. Alone.

"What's going on?" Brandy said, her voice breathless through the phone.

"She got into her car alone," Steph said as she moved around the restaurant.

"Good. Find out what kind of car he drives and get the license plate number."

She froze at this. "Are you serious?"

Lydia's car drove toward her, and she faced the other way so Lydia wouldn't be able to see her face. Once the car passed, Steph moved into the parking lot in time to see mystery man get into a silver truck.

"It's a truck—one of those smaller ones." She continued walking and talking as if she were minding her own business. "A Tacoma." Then she read off the license plate number to Brandy. "Got it?"

"Got it." She sounded triumphant. "I'm pulling up to the sidewalk now."

Once Steph was inside the car, Brandy took off after the silver truck.

"What are you doing?"

"Making sure Greg isn't heading to Everly Falls."

Steph wanted to protest, but she was curious, too. They drove in silence for a few moments until the truck turned down a road that was decidedly not in the direction of their hometown.

"Wow, I can't believe we pulled that off," Brandy said as she made a U-turn. "Do you think my mom saw you when she drove past?"

"I doubt it." Steph pulled off her scarf and folded it. "I was well disguised."

Brandy's laughter sounded with relief. "I can't wait to see who the license plate belongs to."

Just Add Friendship

"Are you taking it to the cops?" Steph asked, surprised.

"I don't know yet." Brandy drummed the steering wheel. "I'll talk to Ian. See what he thinks." She paused. "After what happened with Brock . . . I know I have trust issues."

"Nobody would blame you," Steph hurried to say, and no one would. When Brandy called things off with her former fiancé Brock, he went a little crazy. Okay, so a lot crazy. Resulting in him getting arrested . . . "We'll get a background check, or whatever they're called, and then we'll know."

Brandy squeezed Steph's hand, then returned to the steering wheel. "Thanks for being my wingman and not telling me I'm overreacting."

"Well, I overreacted first, so maybe you're *my* wingman."

Brandy laughed. "Let's just hope that's all this is . . . two friends overreacting."

Steph smiled at her, hoping her friend would think it was genuine. Because seeing Lydia hug that man had bothered Steph more than she wanted to admit to Brandy. And she didn't know why. She really needed to stop reading mysteries.

"Can you do me a couple of favors?" Brandy asked.

"Sure, anything."

"First, you owe me twenty bucks. Second, text Mom in about an hour—ask how the date went. See what she says."

"I can do that." Steph opened up her phone to set a reminder and check the texts that had started to chime in. At the restaurant, she'd had her phone off. Now, she realized she'd missed a huge committee discussion.

"What's up?" Brandy asked.

"Oh, it's about the reunion tomorrow. Looks like the

balloon vendor has a supply issue. We'll only get about half the balloons we ordered. Marci's panicking."

"Oh darn." Brandy smirked. "We'll only have one balloon arch?"

"You know how Marci loves her balloon arches." Marci had been the student body president their senior year, and she was all about balloon arches at every school dance and event.

"Text Everly to see if they have balloons in stock at the craft store," Brandy said.

"Good idea." Steph sent out a quick text.

"Oh, and let me know if you want to be set up with one of Ian's new friends," Brandy added, trying to sound casual again.

"No thanks." Steph straightened in her seat. They'd just reached the outer limits of Everly Falls. "I'm going solo. It might be fun."

"Ah, I was waiting for you to say that."

Steph shot her a glance. "What? Why?"

"Because, you know . . . *he* might be there. The man who must not be named."

Steph laughed, even though her stomach had started doing somersaults. "That's a chance in a million. We don't have any current contact information on him."

"Just his former home address?"

"Yep—so maybe it was forwarded, or maybe not."

"You're hoping though . . ."

Steph brushed off the comment. "I'm curious to know what happened to him, sure, but for no reason other than curiosity."

"Hmm." Brandy slowed in front of the small house with a patchy lawn where Steph lived with her grandpa.

"Just admit it," Brandy said as Steph opened her door.

She paused. "Admit what?"

"That you're dying to see Cal Conner because he was your best kiss ever."

Heat rushed to Steph's neck, but she kept her voice as cool as a melting snow cone. "That might be true, but I've moved on from high school crushes and guys who disappear overnight."

Three

"If you keep looking at the door all night, you're going to have a kinked neck," Brandy teased Steph.

She snapped her gaze to Brandy's as they sat together at a decorated table in their old high school gym. "I'm not—"

"Don't even bother denying it," she said in her too-loud whisper. "You look stunning, by the way. Blue is really your color, and those stilettos are to die for."

"Thrift shop," Steph said, glad for the change of topic. She had no doubt Brandy's hunky boyfriend Ian had heard every word. Steph really needed to mingle anyway, and now was as good a time as any. She pushed up from her chair. "I've gotta say hi to a few people. I'll see you both later."

Ian smiled with a nod, but Brandy grasped her hand. "Text me any updates on my mom."

"Of course." So far, everything Lydia had said had been normal first date stuff. Nothing with red flags. When Steph asked if she'd made a second date, she'd said not yet. So Brandy was taking advantage of that buffer to continue working behind the scenes. The license plate number didn't set off any alarms, since the guy didn't have any tickets or arrest warrants.

Just Add Friendship

As Steph weaved through the gathering, she greeted people, asked how they were doing, and gave her fifteen second spiel of "I'm living with my grandpa and working at the salon. What about you?"

No sign of Cal Conner. And as the minutes ticked by, Steph decided she was glad he hadn't shown up. She could keep his memory as a high school one. Fun, daring, swoony—because yes, that kiss did happen—mysterious, and well, all fantasy. Because who was she kidding. Cal Conner hadn't been her type in high school, and she was pretty sure he still wouldn't be her type.

She worked at a small-town salon, for heaven's sake, and the man she planned to marry—once she met him—would be financially secure. Because she didn't plan on living in her grandpa's rundown excuse of a house for the rest of her life. And Cal Conner, with his longish hair, his beat-up motorcycle, his wrinkled five-dollar bill he'd bought sodas with on their one and only date, his lousy grades, all that time spent in after-school suspension . . . No, he wasn't her type. He was only the token bad-boy high school crush.

"Steph, you haven't changed!" someone said in a singsong voice.

She turned to see a woman who looked very familiar. Dark hair, pretty eyes . . . "Darla! You haven't changed either."

The two women hugged briefly, then Darla introduced her husband, and started talking about her three kids. *Three!* Imagine. Oh, and Steph had fibbed. Darla had totally changed.

After a few minutes of nonsensical catching up, she was on her own once again. The light buffet had been cleared, and about a dozen couples were dancing on the makeshift dance floor, beneath the single balloon arch.

More balloons had been found, but Marci had opted to make balloon trees for table centerpieces, which was cute in theory, but made it hard to have a conversation with anyone across the tables.

Speaking of Marci, she was with her husband-slash-high-school-boyfriend at the display table that sported pictures and memorabilia of Everly Falls High School. Steph had helped set that up, and she knew there was one picture with Cal Conner in it—at a football game. He was a face in the crowd, but Steph remembered that night well because it had been the first time he'd spoken to her.

Marci laughed at something her husband said and wrapped her arms around him. Their easy affection only made Steph feel *more* single, if that were possible. She and Marci had been on the cheer squad together, but Steph's real friend group was made up of Brandy, Lori, and Julie.

Speaking of Julie . . . she and her husband Dave were currently dancing, if a bit awkwardly to account for Julie's pregnant belly. Steph tamped down a laugh. They were an adorable couple. And now, it looked like Brandy and Ian were dancing, too—looking movie-perfect together.

Steph turned away with a half smile. She was happy everyone was having a good time. It was also nice to see former friends, but she felt drained. Lonely in a crowded room, somehow. It seemed like everyone had someone here, either a partner, or at least a date.

It was fine, she told herself firmly. Better that she discovered Nate was still in love with his ex now than find out later. She spent the next hour catching up with former classmates, listening to their life stories—ones she'd probably forget almost immediately. As the evening wound down, she helped with the cleanup even though she wasn't officially on the cleanup crew, and even though her feet were killing her from her stilettos.

Just Add Friendship

There were only a handful of people left in the gym when she left the school. She'd leave it up to the janitor to officially close everything down and lock up. It was a bit surreal to be walking to her car in a mostly empty parking lot. The September night was crisp, and the cool wind helped to clear her head of the millions of conversations she'd had. Thankfully, tomorrow was her day off, and she could luxuriate in bed as long as she wanted.

Well, until Pops was hungry for breakfast.

She released a sigh and climbed into her car. She could have technically walked, but then she would have had to bring a change of shoes. As it was, she dragged off her shoes before starting her car.

The engine clicked, but didn't roar to life. She tried again, but nothing this time. If there was one thing she didn't know how to do, it was mechanical stuff, or yard work, or house repairs . . . but she could do other things—more essential things, like make people feel beautiful.

The third try brought the same result.

"Fine. I'll walk and figure this out in the morning," she said to herself. She grabbed her purse and heels and climbed out of the car, wishing she had a pair of tennis shoes to change into.

Another person had come out of the building, and for an instant, Steph wondered if she could ask for a battery jump, but she was pretty sure it wasn't the battery. That thing was only a few months old. It was probably the starter—and hopefully nothing more serious, although she didn't exactly have money for a new starter either.

She leaned against the car and slipped on her shoes. If the person heading to his car was someone she knew—maybe she'd ask for a ride? Save her feet? It was a man, that had become clear by his size, breadth of shoulders, and long gait.

Before she could straighten and call out to him, he'd veered toward her.

And then she knew.

How she didn't see him inside the gym was beyond her. Because although his hair was short, and he dressed like the full-grown adult he was, everything else was the same. His deep-set brown eyes, his angular jaw, his slow stride like he had all the time in the world . . . his very presence. Creating goose bumps once again on her arms and neck.

"Bee." He said the single word on an exhale.

And then he was standing in front of her. Giving her some space, but also allowing her to notice the changes. She now realized she *had* seen him inside the gym. At a distance. Because she remembered the man in a dark suit and tie. Thought he looked nice, but immediately dismissed him as being someone's date.

"Cal?"

He didn't answer, just gazed at her with those bottomless dark eyes.

"I didn't see you—I mean, I might have seen you, but didn't realize it was you." She waved a limp hand. "You look . . . different."

"It's the hair."

His voice was the same low tone she now remembered. How could she have forgotten? Well, maybe she hadn't. The electricity sizzling through her was a testament that a decade hadn't dulled her reaction to this man. "It's more than the hair. You're . . . wearing a suit?"

One side of his mouth lifted. "I am."

"You are." She needed to get control of her heart rate. And stop stating the obvious. "How have you been?"

His brow arched. "Look, we can skip the small talk. That's what inside the gym was for. Where you were avoiding me—"

"I wasn't avoiding you," Steph cut in. "I didn't recognize you from a distance." Now, up close, she couldn't believe she hadn't recognized him.

He went quiet for a moment, his brow still quirked. "Look, I owe you an apology."

"Just one?" she blurted, nervous.

"Probably a lot of them, but mostly for not telling you the truth."

"About bailing on the prom?"

"Yeah . . . that, too." He slipped out of his suit jacket and moved toward her, then set it across her shoulders. "You're freezing."

Steph couldn't deny it. It was plenty cold tonight. His jacket was warm and smelled . . . like Cal Conner, like the night air. Clean and crisp. He was also standing much closer now, and she knew it wouldn't take her long to warm up.

"What's wrong with your car?" he asked, his gaze flicking past her.

"It won't start."

He stepped past her, and she grabbed his arm. "It's fine. It's not the battery, and I'll just call the mechanic in the morning. I was going to walk home."

He paused and looked down at her hand still on his arm. Then his gaze lifted to hers. "Have you been having trouble before this?"

"Cal, I'm not putting you or anyone else out this late," she said. "But if you really want to help, and maybe that will aid in all your apologies, you can give me a ride home. My feet are killing me."

His gaze held hers for a long moment, and she wondered what he was thinking—what he saw when he looked at her.

"All right," he said, his words sounding careful. "Where do you live?"

"Same place."

Both his brows lifted. "Your pops still kicking around?"

"He is."

"Good man."

Steph scoffed. "That's not what you said when he threatened you."

Cal shrugged. "Wasn't the first time I'd been threatened by an adult." He nodded toward another car in the parking lot. "Let's get you in a warm car."

"I'm not that cold," Steph said, walking alongside him.

He looked over at her—well, down at her, since he'd apparently grown a couple more inches. "You're shivering."

"I'm warming up now."

His laughter was soft, and it buzzed through Steph, feeling like she'd been draped in a warm blanket. She remembered the time when she wondered if he ever laughed, and she remembered the time she'd first heard it.

"You drive a Honda?" She stopped dead before a completely normal-looking sedan.

Cal unlocked the car with his key fob, then opened the passenger side door. "I do. I've been domesticated and tamed."

Steph scanned his person. "By a wife?"

This brought a laugh from him, and she found herself smiling back. "No wife. And no girlfriend if that's your next question. Life has kicked me upside the head a few times, and I guess I finally got smart."

She moved past him to climb into the passenger seat. "Uh, a haircut and a Honda don't completely change a person."

Cal only smiled and shut the door.

As she waited for him to walk around and climb in, she looked about—searching for any clues as to how much of a turnaround Cal did. The car was clean. Mostly. In the back seat were a couple of auto magazines and a box of protein bars. Hmmm.

Cal climbed in and started the engine. The heat came through the vents, warming up by the second, and soon Steph was toasty enough to slip off his suitcoat.

"So, about that apology?" she asked as he steered through the parking lot.

"Didn't think you were going to let me forget that."

Curiosity was raging in her veins, but she carefully folded her arms and said, "I'm listening."

Four

CAL CONNER HAD BEEN DOING a lot of apologizing lately, so what were a few more—especially since Steph Grady deserved every last one. He couldn't help but think if he'd stuck around Everly Falls a while longer, they might have dated—for real. If she had wanted to, of course. Her grandfather was certainly not a fan of his, and Cal didn't blame him in the least.

Cal had been rough around the edges as a teenager—to put it nicely—but he'd learned over the past few months to stop ignoring his past. And most importantly, to be open about who he really was. When people knew the truth, it wasn't such a bad, terrifying thing. They understood, they gave him a second chance, and he'd even found a career he enjoyed and could be successful at.

He'd known about the high school reunion for several weeks, of course, and that's when he'd put his plan into action. If there was one gaping hole in his life, it was Everly Falls. And it was time to put it to rights.

So here he was . . . apologizing. So far tonight, he'd apologized to the principal of the high school, who'd made an appearance at the class reunion. He'd apologized to a couple of teachers he tracked down as well. He apologized to his former classmates where he could—at least the ones he remembered. Everyone had been gracious, forgiving. A few gave him blank stares as if they didn't remember. And maybe they hadn't, but he'd never forget.

Now . . . Steph was one of the important ones—probably the most important one.

They were already on the street where she'd directed him, and he'd have to make it quick. He didn't want to commandeer too much more of her time. Driving her home was a bonus, of course. Steph was still beautiful—hadn't really changed in looks, but there were subtle changes. Her makeup was more natural—not that she needed it. Her hair was a darker red now, more auburn. And she was a bit more curvy. He probably shouldn't admit to noticing that.

He glanced over at her as he slowed in front of her grandpa's house. He hadn't expected to feel such a jolt when he saw her at the reunion. Even in a crowded gym that blared music, he noticed her the second he walked in. How could he not? She was vibrant, beautiful, and drew people to her like a magnet.

He moved his gaze to the yard of the house—the grass was in a sorry state. "Does your grandpa have a blight on his lawn?"

"A blight?"

"Yeah, it's a grass disease."

"I don't know." Steph sounded like she'd never heard of grass problems, when it was clear the yard was in vast need of repair.

"Does he have a yard service, or anything—"

"Look, Cal," she cut in with that pert voice of hers. "I'm where the buck stops. Okay? I do the yard, the house, the shopping, take care of Pops . . . everything. How about we focus on you for a moment."

He almost laughed, but he didn't. Her bluntness was a nice reminder of her fiery personality. "Right. The apologies."

"Right." Her tone softened a tad.

He left the engine idling, but turned off the headlights. "I need to back up to before I came to Everly Falls my junior year. And if it's okay, save your questions until the end?"

Steph nodded.

He took a deep breath. "My mom was killed in a car accident when I was fifteen."

Her eyes popped wide. "What? Oh, Cal, I didn't know."

He continued, even though she'd already interrupted him. "For a while, my dad kept things together, until he didn't. He stopped coming home most nights. I found out later he'd lost his job and was drowning his sorrows in a bottle. The nights he did come home, he picked fights. I was grounded all the time . . . either me, or my cell phone. I kept hoping things would get better—you know, the whole grieving thing would ease up—but that didn't happen."

"Cal . . . I don't know what to say."

He pushed on, because his stomach felt hollow, and this was harder to get through than he'd expected.

"My aunt stopped by for a visit at my dad's. She took one look at the situation and threatened legal action against him, but he didn't even put up a fight. His last words were, 'Take him. He reminds me too much of his mom anyway.' Not long after I moved in with Rachel, she got a job offer at the medical clinic in Everly Falls. So we ended up here."

"I thought Rachel was your mom."

"That's what we let everyone believe," Cal said. "Easier than dealing with a bunch of questions. Deadbeat dad story was all true, though."

"I'm sorry, Cal."

It was nice to hear her sympathy, but he wasn't here for that. He held up a hand. "I'm not looking for sympathy, and I'm not giving out excuses. I just want you to understand and accept my apology."

"Why didn't you tell me about your mom?"

He blew out a breath and closed his eyes. When he opened them again, he said, "I think because it was the only way I was keeping things together—at least in my mind. If I didn't tell anyone about my mom, or what my dad became, then I wouldn't have to feel the pain."

"But it did happen, and you did feel it."

He nodded. "Yeah . . . As good as Rachel was for taking me in, she wasn't exactly available for the raging emotions of little old me. She worked the night shift and was asleep most of the time I was awake. I used to go to detention because I couldn't deal with the empty house and the memories that would plague me when I was alone. At least in detention, I could focus and do homework."

He felt Steph staring at him. "You *purposely* went to detention?"

"Yeah." He glanced at her beautiful face, illuminated by the moonlight. "Messed up, huh?"

But she didn't have the pity in her expression that he'd seen from everyone else he'd apologized to. In fact, it was more akin to anger.

"Cal . . . we were friends. At least we were on our way to becoming friends. And well . . . we got kind of close that last night together."

Yeah, he remembered.

"I told you stuff about *me*. Personal stuff. Yet you were keeping so much inside."

"I know." He sighed. "When you shared personal stuff, I

think it freaked me out a little. It touched things inside of me that I'd been holding in for so long. But I liked you. A lot. I think if we'd gone out again, I might have opened up. You know, I just needed a little more time."

Her brows tugged together. "Where *did* you go?"

That was the big question he needed to answer. It was finally time. "When I got home that night, my dad was there. Sobered up. Ready to take on the responsibilities of a parent again, or so he said. Promised rainbows and happily ever after."

"Wow," Steph whispered. "Was that good or bad?"

"It was the worst thing he could have done," Cal said. "I know that now—but back then, I was conflicted. I'd locked everything about my parents and my past into a box with a combination only I knew. Rachel seemed resigned to letting me go back home. It wasn't like she really had legal guardianship anyway. But it had been nearly a year. I'd started to like Everly Falls, despite my delinquency. I'd started to like you . . . I'd just been hired at the movie theater. I finally felt like a real teenager, and not some messed-up alien who everyone avoided."

Steph set her hand on his arm. Just that small touch was what he remembered. The girl who cared, the girl who seemed to look past all of his walls and defenses and saw right into him—into the heart that was still beating and wanting connections.

He looked down at her smooth fingers on the sleeve of his dress shirt.

"Is that why you left?" she asked in a soft voice. "You went home with your dad?"

He heard the confusion in her tone, but patience and understanding leaked through. He knew she wondered why he couldn't have just texted her. Said goodbye at least. But that had been impossible.

"No." He shifted his arms and linked his fingers together. Her hand dropped away. He was relieved at the loss of her touch—it had been making it harder to focus. "My dad said we'd leave first thing in the morning. Told me to pack up. That night, while he slept on the couch, I let my mind pull up the hard things I'd pushed deep down. It was like Pandora's box had cracked wide open in my head. I remembered the fights, the threats, eating mac and cheese dry out of a box because I was afraid to wake him by turning a light on in the kitchen . . . What Rachel didn't know, and what I never let myself remember, were the times my dad had turned on me. Physically."

"Oh, Cal," Steph whispered.

"When he stood in Rachel's house with apologies and promises, it all seemed too good to be true, you know. Fake somehow." He dragged in a breath and blinked against the burning in his eyes. "I panicked, I guess. Or maybe I thought clearly for the first time since my mom died. I sneaked out of the house with only the clothes on my back and every dollar I could scrape up. Didn't take my cell phone because I didn't want to be tracked."

He could literally see the information sink in, crisscrossing Steph's puzzled expression. "I'm sorry I didn't give you a heads-up or try to contact you later," he continued.

Steph waved a hand. "Cal . . . I don't even know what to say. You ran away? Where did you go? How did you survive?"

He gave her a half smile. "That's a really long story—something to save for another time."

"I'm not in a hurry," Steph said.

He nodded, but pulled out his phone. "Can I get your number? So we don't fall off opposite sides of the planet again."

"All right, then, but this time, don't forget to text me for a decade."

Her comment stole his breath. "Bee, I never forgot. That was far from the issue."

"I know." She studied his face, and he gazed right back.

Just seeing her again was bizarre. When he'd left Everly Falls, she'd been his biggest regret. Sure, he was grateful to Rachel for putting a roof over his head, but his only real connection had been the peppy redhead who talked a mile a minute and wasn't put off by his sullen moodiness.

Now, Steph flashed him a small smile, then grabbed his phone. She put in her number, then called her cell. When her phone rang, she created a contact with his name. "All set." She paused. "Thanks, Cal, for explaining."

"No problem. Tonight I'm telling Rachel everything, too."

"Oh, that's good."

Silence followed, dividing them. She, in a stable small-town life; he, living on the road most of the time. Despite his craving to have something solid, real, he was still a transient, it seemed.

"I'll see you later, I guess?" She popped open the door. "Don't answer that. You don't owe me anything. But I appreciate the explanation, Cal, although you really have nothing to apologize for. You couldn't have predicted your dad's return."

"Yeah, true."

She climbed out of the car, and Cal opened his door, too, because he wasn't quite ready to say goodbye. Wasn't quite ready to never see her again. He walked her to her porch, where the yellow light cast a feeble glow over the cracked cement.

"You know, they have outside LED bulbs that will give the porch more light and last quite a while."

"What are you, a fix-it guy now?"

He shrugged. "I know a few things."

She gazed up at him, her expression open, curious, and if he didn't have to talk to Rachel tonight before he left early in the morning, he'd find a way to spend more time with Steph.

"You take care of yourself, Cal Conner. It's really good to see you again."

"It's good to see you again, too." The words felt stilted, awkward even.

The silence seemed to echo the ten-year silence between them.

Then, she stepped forward and wrapped her arms around his waist, hugging him fiercely.

His heart about jolted out of his chest. He slipped his arms about her, holding her close, and inhaling the scent of her shampoo as pretty much every memory of her hummed through his mind. From the first time he saw her walk into math class with a gaggle of friends, to how she confessed that the only school subject that came easy to her was spelling, which was why he started calling her Bee. And finally, their first, and last, date.

His skin was plenty warm now, even though he'd left his suit coat in the car, and his memories continued. Remembering their kiss that night. How he couldn't stop smiling all the way home. Then, how quickly that smile disappeared when he saw his dad's car in the driveway of his aunt's house.

When Steph's hold loosened, he reluctantly let her go. She stepped back and blinked up at him. "You take care of yourself," she said again.

Her voice sounded shaky, and he tried to think of some reply, but his throat was strangely thick.

She gave him a small smile, and he nodded, then she opened the door. Disappeared inside. Just like that.

It wasn't until he heard the lock of the door click into place that he turned and stepped off the porch. He had more explanations and more apologies awaiting him, but as he walked back to his car, he felt lighter than he had in ten years.

Five

STEPH GREETED HER NEXT CLIENT, Gayle—a spunky seventy-year-old who usually spent the duration of her hair appointments talking about her dog, Oliver. Yep, today was no different. But Steph was grateful for the one-sided conversation because she couldn't quite focus on the reality of the day. She felt like she was still someplace between sleeping and waking up. Saturday night was a dreamlike memory—had it really happened?

The reunion had happened, sure, but the rest of it?

Cal Conner had talked to her, apologized to her, driven her home, traded phone numbers . . . hugged her. Then disappeared again. He'd said he was leaving the following morning after staying at his aunt's.

Steph hadn't really expected to hear from him on Sunday, if he was traveling. But now it was Monday. Surely he was home—wherever that was. She'd been tempted to call or text him, but so far she'd refrained. He *had* promised . . .

"I can't ever say the word 'walk' in Oliver's presence, or he'll go crazy with excitement," Gayle said, her brown eyes warm and bright in the reflection of the mirror as chatter buzzed around them from the other stylists and clients. "He thinks I'm going to take him out—rain or in the dark. Such a silly dog."

Steph smiled as she trimmed Gayle's hair.

"I'm getting him a new leash for his birthday," she continued without missing a beat. "Did I tell you it's tomorrow? He'll be seven years old. Imagine!"

Steph nodded, trying to listen, but mostly failing. Where was Cal now? Where did he live? What was his job? Did he have a girlfriend? He'd been quick to say he didn't. But he was probably dating. Cal had aged in the best way possible, and his lean teenaged body had filled out into a well-built, physically fit man. He'd always been handsome in his broody way. Some of that had lifted with his cleaned-up professional appearance. Surely plenty of women hit on him. Surely he had his pick.

Her phone buzzed with a text. She kept it on the counter next to the blow-dryer in case Pops needed anything. And in case . . . *Cal* texted.

She glanced over at the illuminated screen, but the text was from the group chat. Something about Julie's pre-contractions, called Braxton Hicks. They'd been going on for weeks. Not that Steph knew a lot about pregnancies, but Julie kept them all updated. It was amusing, but only frustration pulsed through Steph right now. She hated waiting on a man. Mostly because she was always disappointed—not at the beginning . . . but in the end. Which was why she was still single.

After Gayle was finished, had paid, and thanked her, Steph took her lunch break. She only had about twenty minutes until the next client, but she decided she was done keeping vigil for Cal's text. So she texted him.

Hi, Cal. Just checking in to see how things went with

your aunt. It was nice to see you the other night, and I hope you have safe travels. Wherever they are.

Friendly, maybe a little chatty, and not too direct. She'd be more direct if they had a phone conversation, but she didn't want to lay everything out in a text.

She hit Send, then unwrapped the turkey sandwich she'd made that morning. It was a decent enough sandwich, but nothing like when one of the stylists made a lunch run to the café. Steph couldn't afford café runs every day, though, so mostly she brought something from home since she made lunch anyway for Pops and put it in the fridge.

Although, twice last week, she'd come home from a long day of work to find out that he hadn't touched the sandwich. Said he forgot to eat. She'd be bringing it up at his next checkup.

Her phone buzzed, and she reached for it. She opened the screen and saw another text from her friend group. Still chatting about Julie's pregnancy. Fine with Steph. Their group texting the day before had been all about the reunion. No one had mentioned Cal Conner. Apparently, Brandy and Julie hadn't recognized him either. Everly hadn't known him because she'd graduated a couple of years earlier than the rest of them. And for some reason, Steph hadn't confessed. It seemed lately she'd been keeping guy issues more to herself. Maybe because she felt like her life was moving backward, while everyone else's was moving forward.

"Just call him," she said aloud to the rows of hair-color products on the shelf in front of her. "If he answers, then fine, if not, then maybe he'll text back . . . or maybe he'll ghost you. But then you'll know."

Okay, now she was talking to herself. She took another bite of her turkey sandwich, then swallowed down some water. She tapped Cal's contact and let the phone ring—each ring like a branding iron poking her skin.

It cut off abruptly, and Steph pulled the phone away and stared at it. He'd sent one of those auto-texts: *Sorry, I can't talk right now.*

She stared at the text for a long moment. Either he really couldn't talk, or he didn't want to talk, and she'd crossed some invisible line of bringing their past relationship into the immediate future. It was one thing for him to apologize at the reunion—but another to continue communicating after he'd rectified their past and moved on.

Had he moved on?

Clearly, he had.

Should she reply to his text? No . . .

One text was enough. And now she wasn't hungry anymore, so she packed up her sandwich. It wouldn't last until the end of her shift, but maybe a little later, she'd finish it off. Once the tangled butterflies in her stomach sorted themselves out.

Another text made her flinch. "Stop doing that," she whispered to herself.

This one was from Lydia Kane: *I have another date with Greg. Thought I'd tell you since you're my only confidante. Maybe if this one goes well, I'll tell the girls.*

Well, that was both good and bad. Good because Lydia really should keep her daughters in the loop, and bad because Steph would again have to break confidence and report to Brandy. Which might prompt another reconnaissance mission. At least it would get her mind off Cal Conner.

Great, what are the plans? she texted.

The dots on the message app danced as Lydia typed out her reply, only to be interrupted by someone calling.

Cal's name lit up the screen.

Steph stared at it. Was he really calling? Should she answer? Of course she should . . . so why was she just staring at her phone like she was in some sort of trance?

Just Add Friendship

She drew in a breath, then another, and answered in a completely mellow, non-breathless voice. "This is Steph. How may I help you?"

There. More professional.

"Hey, sorry I had to cut off your call."

His voice came through the phone as deep, warm, melty . . . Steph leaned forward in her chair. "No worries. I just—well, I'm on a work break and wanted to see how things went with your aunt."

There was a significant pause. Was she being too nosy? Too presumptuous that he'd want to tell her anything? If anyone was a locked box, it was Cal.

"It went fine," he said. "She knew some things already, and it was nice to see her again."

"Good to hear."

Another beat of silence.

Now what . . . "So, where do you live?" she asked at the same moment he said, "Where do you work?"

Steph laughed. Wow, she was nervous.

"I work at Carol's Cuts & Curls," she said. "You know, cutting and styling hair."

"Oh. You do?"

"Don't sound so surprised, Cal." Steph felt cringy inside. "It's a decent and productive job."

"I'm not . . . I didn't mean to . . . Uh, I'm starting over. I just thought you were going to be an English teacher. You were a spelling whiz and also so good at English."

A familiar pang jagged through her chest. That night of their one and only date had been when she'd confessed her dream of going to college and becoming an English teacher . . . things she hadn't even told her best friends. "My work break's not long enough to explain that," she said lightly.

Cal's laugh was warm, and Steph cursed the perky butterflies in her stomach.

"All right, we'll save that for another time."

"And you owe me your stories, too."

"True."

The pause between them felt heavy. "So . . . where do you work? What do you do?"

"I'm a private investigator."

This caused Steph to straighten in her chair. "What? Really?"

"That was enthusiastic." He sounded surprised.

Steph was smiling. "I can't believe it. I have sooo many questions. Wait, what are your rates?"

"What's going on?" His voice went serious. "Are you in trouble, Bee?"

The use of his personal nickname for her got the butterflies twisting and turning again. "Oh, not me, but for someone else. It's . . . complicated."

Someone tapped on the door, and it opened a crack. "Steph? Your two o'clock is here."

"Be there in a sec," she told Ally.

The door shut, and Steph told Cal, "I've got to go, but I really do have questions for you. If that's okay, I mean? Do you have a consultation fee?"

"Don't worry about that," he said in a businesslike tone. "When are you finished for the day?"

"Around six."

"Okay, call me then. I'll make myself available."

She could hardly believe her luck—Cal Conner was a private investigator? She knew she couldn't officially hire one, but maybe just asking a few questions would help her and Brandy ease their minds? "Thanks, Cal."

"Sure thing."

Once they hung up, and Steph had started on her next client—Mrs. Vanderhaven, who only wanted a wash and set—she wondered if there were too many coincidences going on. As in, were things too good to be true? Cal rode in on a white horse just after her breakup with Nate, apologizing. He was in the very profession that could help her out of her dilemma with Brandy and her mom . . . It was as if things were finally lining up and going her way.

She shook those thoughts away. Closure with Cal was nice, but that was all it had been. And it would be good to get a professional's advice.

The rest of the afternoon both crawled and sped by. She headed out of work with only the minimal goodbyes to the rest of the stylists, then walked home.

There'd been a message from the mechanic that her car needed a new starter and would be in the shop for a few days while they waited for the ordered part. The walk home wasn't far, and she'd worn her lower-heeled sandals. The only problem was Pops had a doctor's appointment in a few days, and she needed a car to drive him.

She could borrow one of her friends', she knew, but she hoped it wouldn't come to that.

As she approached the house she'd been living in for several years—caretaking for Pops after her parents retired and moved to Florida—she noticed the patchy brown lawn. Well, she always noticed it, but now, she remembered Cal's words. She needed to research lawn diseases and find out if there was any hope.

Should she wait until next spring, though?

She bypassed the lawn and walked into the house.

"'Bout time you got home, it's freezing in here," Pops said from where he sat at the kitchen table, surrounded by newspapers.

"Love you, too, Pops, how was your day?" She kissed the top of his speckled, balding head.

"Cold."

Steph set her hands on her hips. "You're wearing shorts and a T-shirt. Have you tried to dress like it's September?"

"Shouldn't have to," he retorted. "I'm inside my own house."

Steph let the words roll off—Pops alternated between grumpy and sarcastic.

"Well, how about I make you a hot dinner to warm you up?"

He folded his arms and watched her move about the kitchen. Steph opened the fridge and saw that the sandwich she'd made him was missing—so that was good, at least.

"Does chili sound good?"

"Sure," he grumbled.

His mood would lift after he ate—he was that predictable. At least he wasn't complaining about chili two nights in a row. There was plenty left over from the batch she'd made yesterday. As she heated it on the stove, she popped some bread in the toaster, then put together a quick salad.

"Working on a crossword?" she asked.

"Finished them all," he said, his tone easing.

She knew it probably wasn't ideal for him to be alone all day, but his teacher's pension didn't cover all the bills, and she worked to supplement. There'd been a handful of times over the past year that her parents had brought up assisted living for Pops, but he'd been vehemently against it. And while Steph was still single, it made sense for her to watch out for him . . .

She moved to his side and peered at the crossword in front of him. "What about one of those crossword books? Then you wouldn't have to wait for the newspapers every day."

Pops released a noncommittal grunt, which was better than an outright no. Steph made a mental note to grab one at the convenience store next time she was out.

"What's the story with your car?" he asked.

"Needs a new starter."

Pops's gray brows tugged together. "That's expensive."

"They said they'll give me the best price possible, but they're still waiting for a part."

"Reschedule the doctor visit."

Steph returned to the salad fixings. "Oh, no you don't. I'll borrow a car if we need to. No worries." If there was one thing that put her grandpa in a bad mood, it was "some young doctor telling me what to do."

She dished up the warmed chili as Pops continued to grumble. Once she had him fed and distracted by a baseball game on TV, she'd call Cal. Then later, she'd cajole her grandpa into walking around the block with her.

Six

CAL CLOSED DOWN THE INSTAGRAM app after perusing his latest client request. Lately, it seemed he'd gotten more requests from wives, or husbands, to investigate their spouses. Sometimes for suspected affairs, other times for concealing financial information, and this current one was for an ongoing custody battle.

The details were depressing, but the facts didn't lie. Steve Ross was claiming his wife wasn't using child support money on the kids—but instead taking extravagant vacations while the kids sat home alone that previous summer.

Cal might have taken a slight detour and looked up Steph's Instagram profile. No, he didn't follow her, but her profile was public, so he could see what she'd posted. Most of it was pictures of cuts and colors she'd done for work—"before and after" photos—where she'd tagged the customer. He wondered why the salon didn't have its own account, but that wasn't what he was really interested in. He was curious as to why Steph was still single.

She'd been tagged in group photos, and he examined those. Her arms around men, women, laughing, doing all sorts of activities, but there didn't seem to be any consistency with a single man.

Just Add Friendship

Of all the girls in high school, he thought she'd be the one with a husband and kids and a nice home by the time their ten-year reunion rolled around. She was always surrounded by people—guys and girls. It was why he'd taken forever to talk to her . . . well, she technically talked to him first, but he'd noticed her for months. The fact that she talked to him like he was a normal teen, and not the troublemaker of the town, had made him feel . . . noticed—in the right way.

Cal pocketed his phone and strode to the window of his home office in his town house. He lived about an hour's drive from Everly Falls. Kind of ironic, he knew. But the town of Grandin had become a refuge after he'd taken off that night from his dad's fake promises. Cal found his way to an all-night café, and the owner—Donna—had taken him under her wing. Literally.

Fed him, asked him questions, told him that he could sleep on the cot in the back room if he was looking for a place to stay.

He stayed. Donna gave him a job washing dishes. Then she gave him an old laptop—told him to finish up his schooling online. It was a strange few months, working during the day, taking online classes at night. Not spending time with kids his own age. The teens who came into the café seemed curious about him, but Donna just told them he was her nephew.

Cal became a professional people-watcher as he took on more jobs at the café. Cashier, busboy, occasional cook. He knew the exact times the regulars would shuffle in. He became intrigued with people's habits, quirks, and emotions. Like that one time when Mrs. Johnson had bloodshot eyes, and her hands trembled when she drank her coffee. And Mr. Parker, who always left four quarters as a tip.

The town was growing, though, and his newer town house was a testament to that. He adjusted the blinds to let in more of the orange and pink sunset that splashed the sky. Without checking the time, he knew it was after six. After when Steph said she'd call. It wasn't like he was counting the minutes, but the way she acted when he told her his profession had started a knot of worry in his gut. Women like Steph—vivacious, friendly to everyone, easygoing, beautiful, trusting of others—could become easy targets.

When his phone rang, he pulled it out, hoping it was her at last.

"Hey," he said, trying to keep his tone mellow.

"Hi, Cal," she said. "I'm glad you're not screening me anymore."

He chuckled at that. "I'd rather screen than have a three-second conversation to tell someone I need to call them back."

"Oh, I understand. Especially since you probably have a lot of top-secret stuff you're doing."

"Not too top secret. Well, except for whichever current client I'm working for. They're not splashing their information all over the internet." He didn't want to get off topic. He had some questions for her. "What's going on, Bee? Why did you ask for a consultation?"

"It's probably nothing," she rushed to say, although he heard the tension in her voice. "Do you remember Brandy Kane?"

Cal blinked. The name sounded familiar . . . "Oh yeah, your blonde friend who was a freak at math?"

She laughed, and he found himself smiling, easing up just a little. If this was about Brandy, and not Steph, then he could relax more.

"Her mother is dating again—she's been widowed for a

while." Steph paused. "Anyway, I cut Lydia Kane's hair, and she told me about meeting a man on a dating app."

Cal moved to his desk and opened up a document on his laptop. "I'm putting you on speaker." He began to type notes as Steph filled him in on how she and Brandy stalked the date to a Mexican restaurant in another town. Brandy had the man's license plates ran, but nothing came up.

"Wait, you sat in the same restaurant and didn't get caught by Brandy's own mother?"

"Yeah, I didn't think it would work," Steph said. "Brandy brought these scarves."

"I should hire you," Cal said with a laugh. "Or Brandy."

He heard the smile in her voice when she said, "Well, if I ever get tired of cutting hair..."

"And so you know, a license plate report will only show information about the owner of the car and any arrest warrants out for that person."

"Yeah, and Brandy doesn't want to go too far yet, because if things are fine, and her mother found out..."

"I get that."

"Besides, Lydia has another date with the man tomorrow night. Same little town—at the movie theater, I guess. Kind of strange because Everly Falls has a beautifully renovated theater here."

"But Lydia is still trying to keep this guy a secret," Cal mused, "so she's probably not offering her town."

"True."

He typed the name and license plate number Steph had given him into one of his databases. It didn't take long to start a search trail on the man.

"It's probably all innocent, but there's something about him that bothers both of us—and I don't know if it's just because Lydia's keeping him secret. Or that he's quite a bit younger."

"Look," Cal said, pausing in his typing. "I'd be the first person to tell you to trust your gut. We can all talk ourselves out of almost anything. But go with your initial instinct. I can do a few record runs on him and see if anything strange comes back."

"How much would that cost?"

Cal almost smiled. "Nothing."

"Cal, this is your job. I can pay for those record runs. I probably can't pay for a full investigation, but it would be nice to know a little more than the guy's lack of traffic tickets."

He leaned back in his chair. "Let's do this: I'm going to be in your area this coming weekend, and I can bring you whatever I find. Free of charge."

"You're coming to Everly Falls again?"

"Yeah, I told Rachel I'd help her clean out her garage."

Steph didn't speak for a moment. "That's pretty domestic—do you live close?"

"Grandin." He let her process that, then said, "I can stop by when you get off work. What's your schedule like?"

"I work a half day on Saturday, then I have Sunday off." She paused. "I can fix you dinner. Do you want to invite Rachel?"

"Uh, maybe? I'd have to check with her."

"And you owe me a story—you know, about what happened when you disappeared on me."

"That would have to be a private conversation, since I only told Rachel the basics."

Steph's voice went quiet. "Come for dinner on Saturday, and after, we can go for a walk or drive once Pops is fed and watching baseball."

Cal was glad she couldn't see his smile. This was working out quite nicely. "Deal."

Just Add Friendship

After hanging up with her, Cal wondered if he was doing the right thing—pretending he was going to already be in town. Well, he'd better make his white lie into the truth. He sent Rachel a text: *Remember I said I could help with your garage? How does this Saturday work?*

Then he returned to his laptop screen, where a few interesting things had popped up on Greg Makin. Cal followed each of the leads when he had time throughout the week. By the time Saturday rolled around, he had plenty of information on Greg Makin that would send a normal woman running for the hills. He didn't know what sort of woman Lydia was, but the information was definitely something that needed to be shared. Over the past few days, he and Steph had texted quite a bit, and Cal found that he'd enjoyed it. Which only confirmed why he was heading to Everly Falls again, with Steph on his agenda.

She told him her car had been fixed and was back to running, so when he drove past her house early Saturday morning and it was gone, he knew she was at work. He decided it wouldn't hurt to get a closer look at the lawn. He parked in front and strode onto the grass. Plucking a few wilted blades, he examined them, then scuffed his shoe on the ground. The grass practically disintegrated. Maybe he could stop at the hardware store and get a fungicide treatment.

He continued on to Rachel's and was greeted by hot coffee and bagels, neither of which he turned down.

"You know, some of your mother's stuff is in here," Rachel said as she pushed the garage door up, then wiped her hand on her jeans. Her dark hair was pulled into a clip, and tired lines marked her face. She was still working night shifts, but she said she preferred that to day shifts.

"Really?" Why hadn't Cal ever known that? Rachel was his dad's sister, so why would she have his mom's stuff?

"Yeah, your dad gave me her old clothing and a bunch of personal items." She put her hands on her hips as she surveyed the stacked boxes and old furniture. "You can see if you want anything."

The morning became a surreal kaleidoscope of memories as Cal went through the boxes of his mom's stuff. He separated out a few things, such as some of her jewelry pieces and a box of mementoes he remembered her sharing with stories of her childhood.

"Is that all you want?" Rachel asked.

"Yeah, I don't have room for furniture or anything like that." He loaded his mom's things into the trunk of his car, then he set about loading the neighbor's borrowed truck with the rest of what Rachel was donating to the thrift store.

After he made that run to drop off furniture and boxes, he returned to Rachel's to find her sweeping out the garage. She pointed to the rest of the boxes that she'd sorted and labeled. "Can you put those on the shelves—now that there's actually room?"

"Sure thing." Cal complied, and within another thirty minutes, the garage was completely cleaned out, and Rachel's car fit inside.

"Lunch?" she asked. She looked like she was about to drop. Working all night, then cleaning all morning . . .

Cal didn't want to be the reason she couldn't catch a nap. "I'll grab a sandwich later. Thanks for the offer, though."

"No, thank *you*, Cal." She waved a hand. "For coming out to help me. I've wanted to do this for a long time."

He nodded. "Anytime. I mean it. I know I've been incognito for a long time, but I want that to change. You helped me out when I needed it most, and—"

"I shouldn't have let your father come back that night,"

Rachel cut in. "I'm sorry, Cal. I'm sorry that you felt trapped, and then you thought your only solution was to run."

Cal swallowed against the dryness in his throat. "It was all a long time ago. I don't know if I made the right decision that night, but it's in the past now."

Rachel wiped her reddened eyes. "Don't be a stranger." She stepped close and hugged him tight.

He returned the hug. "I won't, and make sure you're getting plenty of sleep."

She laughed and pulled away. "I could say the same thing to you."

After leaving Rachel's, Cal went to the hardware store. He picked up a handful of things that he thought would help with a certain lawn. He'd be early to Steph's, but he was hoping to get a treatment on the grass. Or at least talk to her about it. But when he arrived at her house, he was surprised that her car wasn't there yet. It was well into the afternoon, but maybe she was running errands?

He knocked on the door, and after several moments, it was cracked open. "I'm not buying anything, so you can take your solar panels and—"

"Hello, sir. It's Cal Conner. A friend of Steph's."

The door opened another inch. "Who?"

"Cal Conner. I used to live here when we were both in high school." The memory might not do him any favors.

The door opened wider now, and a wrinkled face topped by a mostly bald head stared out at him. "You that boy with the motorcycle?"

"Yes, sir, or at least I was. I don't have it anymore."

The old man craned to look past Cal, and he stepped aside to make it easier.

"You drive a Honda?"

"Yes."

The man's face crinkled into what he guessed was a smile. "Grown up, have you?"

Cal nodded. "You could say that."

"Well, then, what are you doing here? Steph has a boyfriend, you know."

This was news to Cal, but he tried not to let it show on his face. "That might be, but your granddaughter invited me to dinner, and I thought I'd put on this lawn treatment first."

The man eyed him. "Dinner, huh? She didn't say anything to me."

Cal didn't have an answer for that, so he picked up the bag at his feet. "Mind if I treat your lawn? It won't take very long."

"What are you going to charge?"

"No charge," he hurried to say. "Like I said, it won't take long."

The old man's white eyebrows arched. "Then what are you waiting for? The sun's gonna set in a few hours."

"I'll get right on it." Cal hid a smile and turned to step off the porch.

"You Rachel's kid?"

He paused and turned back. "She's my aunt."

The admission didn't seem to surprise him. "She's a good gal. Treats me right. Now, the doctor's treatment is another story."

"I agree, she's a good lady, and I'll let her know you said hi."

"Hmph." Pops stepped back and shut the door.

"Well, I guess that's my signal to get to work," Cal mused. He pulled out his phone to text Steph that he was at her house, but there was already a text from her.

I'm working a little longer since one of the stylists called in sick. Dinner at six?

He decided to let his early arrival be a surprise, so he wrote back: *Sounds good.*

The lawn treatment was done in less than an hour, and when he knocked on the door again, this time Pops opened it right away. Had he been watching out the window or something?

"Did you change your mind about charging me money?" the old man asked.

"No, sir, I wondered if I could wash up," Cal said. "Then I've got an extra light bulb in my car that I could replace your porch light with."

"You can call me Pops, everyone does." He looked up at the porch light as if it were on at that moment. "It still works."

"Barely."

"Come in." Pops moved out of the doorway and led the way to the kitchen through the front room.

Inside, the place was clean, but it was well lived-in and the furniture well used. Reminded him of Donna's place. Bookcases lined one wall, double and triple stacked with books. Mysteries, historicals, romances, fantasy novels . . . Pops's? Or Steph's?

Once in the kitchen, Cal turned on the kitchen faucet and found the handle loose. After washing his hands, he grabbed a paper towel to dry them.

"How long has the faucet been leaking?" he asked Pops, because the man was sitting at the table watching him like a hawk.

"It drips a little, but only at night."

Cal blinked. It was dripping at that moment. "Maybe you can only hear it at night, but it's definitely dripping."

Pops waved a hand. "Oh, Steph adjusts it when I bug her about it. I don't mind a little dripping. I'd fix it myself, but my eyes aren't what they used to be. And Steph has to watch those dang videos on her phone to do anything around here."

"Videos?"

"She calls them U-Soup."

It took Cal a second. "YouTube?"

"That's it."

He chuckled. "Those are hit and miss. But I've found some good stuff once in a while. I'll get that light bulb changed out, then I'll take a look at the faucet."

"Suit yourself," Pops grumbled.

Seven

STEPH HAD EXACTLY TEN MINUTES to get in and out of the grocery store. Otherwise they'd be eating an hour late. She wouldn't be surprised if Cal was already at her house—probably in an argument with Pops. He argued with everyone nowadays. It used to be he'd only exhibit grumpy behavior at home, but now he wasn't selective at all.

Of course, being Saturday afternoon, everyone in town and their dog—literally—seemed to be out and about. She had to brush off three conversations just to make it to the checkout line under her deadline. Why hadn't she shopped the night before and avoided all of this?

Oh yeah, because she was hanging out with her friends at dinner at the café, and they'd chatted until closing time. Then she'd gone home, turned off all the lights that Pops had left on, and settled into bed to read for a couple of hours. Bliss. But now she was paying for it because she'd ended up covering Eliza's appointments today.

Normally, she would have just rescheduled them all, but she really needed the money to pay off the repair on her car.

When she pulled into the driveway, she wasn't exactly surprised to see Cal's car parked in front of her house. It was nearly six p.m., the time when dinner should have been ready. Steph climbed out of her car, grabbed the groceries from the back seat, then headed to the front door. She grappled to get the knob turned, and when she swung the door open, she saw two men sitting at the kitchen table, playing a card game.

It took Steph a moment to fully take in the image of her grandpa laughing, and the image of Cal sitting in her kitchen.

"Hello?" she said.

When Cal spotted her, he shot up from his chair. "Let me get those bags."

She was still too stunned to do much else but hand them over. At the reunion, he'd been dressed in business attire, but now . . . he looked more like the guy she remembered from high school. Worn jeans, fitted gray T-shirt that showed he wasn't a man of leisure, but one who worked out plenty. His dark eyes flitted over her, and she wondered what he saw—what he was thinking. But she didn't have time to analyze the zooming butterflies in her stomach.

She shut the front door, then headed into the kitchen, where Cal was making himself quite at home by unloading the grocery bags.

If Steph wasn't in such a hurry to get dinner started, she might have just stood in the middle of the kitchen and watched Cal at his domestic chore.

"Chicken fettucine and salad?" he asked, looking over his shoulder at her.

Oops. He'd caught her staring. Ogling, more like. "Yep, sorry I'm later than planned. The chicken is precooked, so it won't take long."

"No problem," Cal said at the same time that Pops announced, "I'm about to wither away like one of those dead grapevines in the backyard."

Steph smirked and crossed over to him. "Great to see you, too, Pops. Oh, how was my day? Long and tiring. How was your day? Full of fun and relaxation." She kissed the top of his head, then looked up to see Cal grinning at her.

She allowed a small smile, but only because his own smile was doing jumpy things to her pulse.

"I'll tell you what was fun," Pops said. "Watching your friend Mr. Conner fix the back door so it doesn't stick anymore, clean out the leaves from the rain gutters—although I thought he was going to topple over on that rusty ladder—replace the kitchen faucet, and get us a brand-new shiny light bulb for the front porch. Oh, and he put something on our lawn so that grass will start growing again."

Steph's gaze moved from Cal to the kitchen sink—the faucet was gleaming, definitely new—then back to him. "You replaced the faucet and . . ."

"I showed up a little early, and Pops put me to work."

Steph spun toward her grandpa. "Pops!"

Her grandpa raised his hands as if he were innocent of any wrongdoing. "He started it—offered to treat the grass, then it went from there."

Cal chuckled. "One thing led to another."

"What, why?" She glared at Pops. "Cal's not a repair guy—he's our guest." She looked at Cal. "How much do we owe you for all the supplies and labor?"

"Nothing," both men said at once.

Steph felt like the air was being squeezed out of her body. "Cal. Can I talk to you for a second? Outside?"

His brows rose, and his mouth quirked. His look of amusement wasn't doing her heart rate any favors.

"You're in trouble now, kid," Pops said with delight as Cal followed her out the back door that had truly been repaired. It didn't stick, and there was no creaking or squeaking or whining as she pulled it shut.

They stood beneath the arbor that had once been intertwined with beautiful grapevines, but had morphed into coarse brown twigs. Steph folded her arms. "What's going on? Why are you doing all this stuff? You don't owe me anything. Just because you felt guilty about ghosting me in high school doesn't mean you need to show up and fix a bunch of stuff. Besides, I was going to get around to all of it. The salon has been extra busy, with the fall festival coming up and the holidays around the corner." She dragged in a breath, so she didn't hyperventilate.

"Are you done?" His voice rumbled with amusement.

She narrowed her eyes. "Maybe."

"I'd like to explain."

She sighed. "Explain."

Humor filled his brown eyes. "I finished at Rachel's and decided to come over to see about the lawn, thinking I could maybe help out while waiting for you to get off work. You know, as a surprise. But one thing led to another—just like your grandpa said."

"Okay, then . . ." She puffed out a breath. "Then how much do I owe you?"

Cal rested his hand on her shoulder. "Nothing, Bee," he said in a lowered tone. "It was no trouble."

She tried to ignore the warmth of his touch and the goose bumps it brought. She was also trying to ignore his clean soap scent, which lingered even though there must have been plenty of exertion on his part today. "At least tell me how much you spent on the lawn treatment and the faucet and the light bulb."

"Probably as much as your groceries for dinner," he said, dropping his hand, and taking the warmth with him.

"Let's not debate pennies. I'd rather make dinner. I'm starving, and your grandpa is, too."

"You're not helping." She rubbed the back of her neck. "It's the least I can do—make you dinner like I said I would."

Cal leaned close, his body invading her carefully arranged space. "You're a stubborn woman. I want to help. In fact, I insist on it."

At the close distance, she could see the lighter browns in his otherwise dark eyes. "You're pretty stubborn yourself."

He smiled, and she felt that smile all the way to her toes.

Which meant it was time for this little tête-à-tête to end. She reached for the doorknob, but he grasped her hand, stopping her.

He released her hand quickly, but the warmth remained. "Wait," he said. "I need to tell you something about your friend's mother. About fifteen minutes before you came home, I got the emailed reports I'd requested. The man she's dating has been married four other times. All to women at least a dozen years older than him. All divorces. I couldn't find any records other than standard divorce proceedings. Without you giving me full access to investigate, I don't know much beyond that. But in my opinion, Lydia Kane should stay away from Greg Makin."

Steph's breath had gone shallow as she stared at him. "Oh wow. I can't believe it . . ." She leaned against the door, her mind spinning around all sorts of conclusions. "Do you think he's a con artist? I mean, that's a lot of divorces . . . right?"

"I don't have proof of him being a con artist—but I could probably get it if you really want."

"No, I think what you've found out is plenty. Bottom line, he's not the man for Lydia." Steph looked up and met his steady gaze. "Thanks for finding that information." She paused. "Would you . . . oh, never mind."

"I'll start dinner, and you call Brandy."

She hated to put another thing on him, because they were all hungry, yet she was dying to tell Brandy as soon as possible. So while Cal played the hero once again, she slipped into her bedroom and reported everything.

"I need to confront Mom," Brandy said into the phone, her voice tight. "She's not going to be happy with me interfering."

"I'm the one who told you when she asked me to keep it a secret," Steph said. "I can send her an apology later—just let me know how she reacts."

"I will," Brandy said. "And Steph, thank you. I'm going to call Everly and update her on everything, because I want her to come with me to Mom's."

"Good idea." When Steph hung up with her friend, she stood in the middle of her bedroom, processing all that had been set into motion with Lydia agreeing to date a stranger she'd met through a dating app. It could happen to any of them. Steph had met men that way . . . She'd given up on apps a while back, and now she was so grateful she had.

Voices rumbled from the kitchen, along with the murmuring sounds of a baseball game. Was the television on? The smell of something delicious cooking made her stomach grumble. She'd have to think more about Cal Conner later—and ask herself why he'd come over early, and stayed, and done so much, and helped her with the information about Greg Makin, and basically been an amazing man.

Opening the bedroom door, she headed down the hall.

Pops was sitting at the table still, but he was tearing up lettuce for the salad. Steph couldn't remember the last time he'd helped with dinner. Oh sure, he'd do cleanup if he was "steady on his legs," but preparing food had never been something he'd volunteered to do.

Just Add Friendship

Cal had the chicken heating in a frying pan, sizzling away, and water boiling the fettucine. And on the corner of the counter, the ancient mini-TV was on—broadcasting the game. That TV hadn't worked for years. Pops usually watched the flat-screen in the living room.

"You got the TV to work?" She crossed to the counter.

"Your boyfriend here wrangled it back to life."

"He's not my boyfriend, Pops." Steph felt Cal's gaze on her. She wouldn't look over at him. Not now.

"I took the back off and shot a little air into it," Cal said.

"Oh, he did more than that," Pops declared. "Spent a good hour fiddling with that thing."

Cal chuckled, and Steph looked over at him then. "Where did you learn to fix so many things?"

"It's a long story," he said, his brown eyes locked on hers.

Here he was, in her kitchen, cooking . . . and her pulse was leaping all over the place.

"How long?" She tilted her head, waiting.

"Well, maybe not that long. It's pretty simple, actually. My dad taught me a lot of the stuff . . . before, you know, my mom died," he said in a soft voice, just above the sound of the baseball game. "It was our thing on the weekends. Fixing up stuff in our house or helping a neighbor. Always made me feel happy I could fix something that had been broken with my own hands and a little bit of time."

"Yeah, well, you definitely have a knack for it." She dragged her gaze from him and began slicing the couple of tomatoes she'd bought.

"Everything go all right with your friend Brandy?" he asked.

Steph glanced at her grandpa. He was focused on the game as he slowly tore the lettuce.

"Brandy is going to fill in her sister, Everly, on all of it," she told Cal. "Then they'll visit their mom in person and talk to her."

He nodded, his expression sober. "Good. I'm glad Brandy is taking this seriously."

Steph grabbed the cucumber and began peeling it. "Me too. Thanks again, Cal." She gave him a sideways glance. He'd turned his attention back to the chicken.

"Anytime."

She knew he was being nice . . . and she more than appreciated it. But she couldn't let his actions and words and general appearance invade her thoughts too much. He'd be leaving tonight, and who knew when she'd see him again? Maybe they'd connect down the road if he visited his aunt again.

Other than that . . . Steph couldn't really expect a long-distance friendship. What would really be the point of that? Unless she had more private investigation questions, or he needed some favor for his aunt?

"Is there a colander around here?" Cal asked, bending to look through a lower cupboard.

"Right here." Steph moved next to him and reached into a higher cupboard, brushing against Cal in the process. He didn't move out of the way like she expected him to. Okay, then . . .

She ignored the warmth zooming through her and set the colander in the sink. Cal drained the pasta, and Steph mixed the chicken into the heated alfredo sauce.

In moments, they had everything dished up, and Pops filled up water glasses for everyone. He was certainly on his best behavior by leaving the soda in the refrigerator. It was a standard argument each night that Steph had with him. No soda for dinner. It wasn't that she wanted to boss him around, but when he drank it, invariably, he'd be up in the middle of the night with raging heartburn. And Steph would have to hear all about it.

"Grace?" Pops said.

Steph almost fell off her chair. She schooled her expression and said, "Sure." Then she folded her hands atop the table.

Pops said a very short prayer and finished with, "Amen."

Cal's voice echoed the amen, and they all dug in.

Well, the men did. Steph was still recovering from her pops's apparently 180-degree change in temperament. Had she walked into another dimension? If so, she preferred this one a lot more than the previous one.

Eight

Cal hadn't missed Steph's surprise—it seemed that she felt it all evening. Which of course made him wonder if Steph ever had help from anyone at all. Yeah, he'd worked on several things at her house, but she seemed genuinely stunned that he was helping to cook, and that Pops was helping as well.

Pops currently sat in the recliner in the front room, the baseball game transferred to the flat-screen, while Cal helped Steph with the dishes. They washed them by hand because she said the dishwasher was having issues.

"I can look at the dishwasher," he offered.

"Oh, no you don't," Steph said. "It probably needs to be replaced. Wouldn't be worth the cost of repair. Besides, we don't normally have a ton of dishes with just the two of us."

Cal set down the dish towel he'd been drying with. "If I look at it, there's no charge. Maybe it's a simple fix—"

"Stop." She set a soapy hand on his arm. "I'm grateful for all your help, but I'm not going to ask you for more. You have your own life."

He looked down at where they touched, and she withdrew her hand.

Just Add Friendship

"Sorry, didn't mean to get you wet."

Cal didn't mind in the least. The adult version of Steph was fascinating. Through her Pops earlier, and over the past hour, he'd learned more about her than he'd known in high school. She was fiercely independent, frugal to the hilt, protective of her grandpa, loyal to her friends, and well, gorgeous. Maybe not in the fashion magazine way, but her blue eyes sparkled with humor, and he found the splash of freckles across her skin adorable. She was quick to smile, quick to laugh, and didn't hold back her opinions.

He also really loved the dress she was wearing. He wondered if she wore dresses to work most of the time. He was surprised that she hadn't changed after getting home, not that he was complaining. Her dark blue dress with polka dots was full in the skirt and swished about her legs as she worked in the kitchen.

He probably shouldn't be checking her out so much. They lived in different towns, and their worlds were miles apart. Besides, he was a tried-and-true loner. He couldn't picture himself with a future that included a gaggle of other people, which a wife and kids and in-laws would turn out to be. *Whoa...* he needed to reel in his thoughts.

"What's the story with your grandpa?" he asked quietly. "I thought you just lived with him, but it's obvious you're his caretaker."

Steph handed him the last dish to dry and turned off the water. "My parents retired to Florida and invited him to go with them. He wanted to stay here—in the house that he lived in and was married in and raised kids in. Not that I blame him, but he has more bad days than good ones, so I don't like being too far out of reach."

"How long have you lived with him?"

"Going on six years now."

"Wow, that's a while," Cal said. "Do your parents come back for visits and to help you out?"

"Not particularly," she said. "I don't know if you remember, but my grandpa is actually my step-grandpa. My mom wasn't too happy when her mom divorced and remarried, so she doesn't have a close relationship with him. I'm the closest one in the family to him."

He heard something in her voice he was pretty sure she was trying to keep hidden. "Is all this stuff with your grandpa why you didn't go to college?"

Her gaze flew to his. "No . . . I mean, it might have been a factor, but not the whole reason."

Leaning against the counter, he asked, "What's the whole reason?" When her face reddened, he wondered if he was being too nosy, but it was too late to take back the question.

"My grades took a dive the last semester of school, so getting a scholarship was out." She leaned against the counter as well, not meeting his gaze. "It's fine. I actually love working at the salon, and I get to help my grandpa. Plus, my best friends are all here. And I can feed my love for English and grammar by reading great books. I've even had a couple of indie authors ask me to do some proofreading. What more could a girl want?"

He opened his mouth to reply, but she cut in. "Do not say what I think you're going to say, Cal."

He feigned innocence. "What do you think I'm going to say?"

"That I need a man."

Cal chuckled. "Uh, I wasn't going to say that."

"Liar."

He nudged her shoulder with his, because somehow he'd inched closer to her in the past couple minutes. "Okay, I am curious, though. I thought you'd be married, maybe with a couple of kids."

She scrunched her nose. "Life doesn't always follow Plan A or Plan B, you know."

"Oh, I know."

"Sorry." Her blue eyes landed on him, regret filling them. "I didn't mean—"

"It's fine." He shrugged it off because they were talking about her, not him. "You're an amazing woman, Bee, so it's hard to believe someone hasn't snatched you up."

She bit her lip, which didn't cool down any of the heat that was rising through Cal's body being this close to her. "I just haven't found the right man, I guess. The last guy I dated hightailed it back to his old girlfriend."

"Well, I'd never be that type of problem."

She turned fully toward him, her lips curving. "Oh yeah? No ex-girlfriend lurking around the corner?"

"No. Nothing like that."

She nodded, then tipped her head. "Wanna go for a walk? You owe me a big, long story."

"Is your grandpa all right alone this time of night?"

"Sure. He'll watch the game until the bitter end. I usually have to cajole him into bed."

After Steph informed her grandpa they were going on a walk, and he replied with, "Stay out of trouble, you two," they were out the door. She had pulled on a jacket, and he grabbed his from his car.

"Are you staying overnight or driving back tonight?" Steph asked, her hands deep in her pockets.

The cool fall air was crisp, but not too cold. The bright moon easily lit the sidewalks where the neighborhood streetlights didn't reach.

"I'll drive back tonight. I'm a night owl. Besides, I don't love staying at Rachel's. Too many memories."

Steph nodded. "I get it." She fell quiet.

How did she do that? Commiserate, yet give him space? He knew it was his turn, and he knew what he'd promised, but suddenly he felt nervous.

"I really had no plan when I left that night," he finally said. "All I knew was that I couldn't go back with my dad, and I was pretty sure that staying at Rachel's would only make everything too messy."

"You were just a kid, Cal," Steph murmured. "I wish you would have asked me for help."

He glanced over at her. She'd taken her hair down, and it tumbled over her shoulders, catching the moonlight. "You were a kid, too. It wasn't like I could ask you to hide me in your attic."

Her smile was ironic. "You're probably right. But I can't believe you were literally homeless."

"Not for long." He told her about the diner and how Donna took him under her wing. He told her how he'd graduated through online school and eventually started at college—although he dropped out and pursued several jobs. All short term. Until he began to work for a private investigations firm. "About a year ago, I struck out on my own."

"And you're still in Grandin? Is Donna around?"

"No—she passed away. One of her nephews took over the diner."

"I'm sorry."

"She was a good woman."

They fell silent again, until Steph said, "And your dad?"

Cal blew out a breath. "That's complicated. A couple of weeks after I left, Donna made me call Rachel and let her know I was safe. Which I did. I told Rachel she could let my dad know that I was fine, but I didn't want to see him."

Steph slipped her arm in his. He wasn't sure if it was because it was dark in this patch of the neighborhood, or if... "But you saw him again, right?"

"Right." He looked up at the night sky. "About three years ago."

Steph slowed their step. "You waited that long?"

"Rachel told me he was sick—cancer." He paused. "I went to visit him in the hospital. And a few weeks later, I went to his funeral."

Steph stopped, which stopped him, too. "Oh, Cal, I'm so sorry."

He looked down at her upturned face. The people who'd come to his father's funeral had told him they were sorry about his dad, but none of it had felt real at the time. He'd been numb to their condolences. Steph's words felt genuine, though.

His throat went tight, surprising him that he was feeling all those emotions again. "It's been three years now, and I can't go back and change anything."

"Would you want to if you could?"

He hesitated. That was a loaded question that he couldn't fully answer. "I don't know. I was coping in my own way, I guess."

She moved her arm from his and grasped his hand. Her fingers were smooth and cool. Soft and comforting. "What did you talk about in the hospital?"

"Not much." He tightened his fingers around hers. He appreciated the comfort. "We never went *there,* and it all stayed superficial. I told him about my job and about where I was living. He didn't ask for any explanations—maybe he'd heard enough from Rachel. But he also didn't apologize." He cleared his throat because it was burning. "And I didn't either."

"He was sorry," Steph said in a quiet voice. "I know it."

Cal blinked against the stinging in his eyes. "Maybe."

She studied him for a second, then she stepped closer and wrapped her arms about him. Just like she'd hugged him the night of the reunion. Cal pulled her close, quicker to act this time, because he suddenly didn't want to miss out on anything she was offering.

He rested his chin atop her head and closed his eyes, breathing in the scent of her shampooed hair. "It's easy to believe my father had regrets when you say it," he murmured.

"How could he not? You were a great kid, and your dad just didn't have the tools to provide for you in the way you needed."

"You're being very generous, to both of us."

"Hmm, maybe."

He heard the smile in her voice.

She nestled even closer, which he didn't mind at all. "I missed you, Cal."

Suddenly all those other things didn't matter as much—his dad's rages, the months spent lonely in a new town, being on the run, trying to figure out a new life in Grandin . . . All of that seemed far in the distant past.

Steph was here, right now. She was real. And she was in his arms.

"Steph, I'm really sorry about disappearing on you."

"I know," she murmured. "And you don't need to keep apologizing. I should be the one saying sorry. You were going through a lot of stuff—things I couldn't even imagine. I should have been nicer."

Cal scoffed. "I think you were the only one in the entire town of Everly Falls to see past my defenses."

She drew away then, her chin raised. "You still have them."

She was right, but it felt like they were melting away with every moment he spent with her.

Steph raised one of her hands, and her fingers traced along his jaw. His pulse responded with backward flips.

"Steph . . ." he whispered, moving his hands to her hips. "I don't want to bulldoze my way into your life again."

The edge of her lovely mouth lifted. "You're in Everly Falls, so I think it's too late for that, Cal Conner." Her hand slipped behind his neck, and he leaned into her pull.

To be closer. To maybe . . . kiss her. Was that what she wanted? He didn't have to question himself about that. There were so many reasons to not kiss her, but right now he couldn't remember a single one of them.

He had to know, though. "Have you been waiting for me?"

She laughed, and it was a beautiful sound. "You still have an ego, I see. I haven't been waiting for anyone. Like I said, I'm perfectly happy in my small-town life."

He was hoping for a different answer. "And you don't need a man?"

"I don't." Her smile grew. "But I really do like icing on cake."

His gaze moved to her mouth, then back to her eyes. "Hmm. What kind of icing?"

"This kind." She lifted up to meet him halfway because he was already bending to kiss her.

He wasn't going to waste another second of this night, not with Steph in his arms and looking at him like he was someone she wanted to spend more time with. Her mouth was cool with the night air, but that changed in about two seconds, and soon it matched his in heat.

He still remembered their first kiss—ten years ago. But now, he realized, he hadn't fully appreciated it. Teenaged kissing was like a fiery, frenzy burst that was over way too fast, followed by confusion and a bunch of questions. *Does she like me? How much? Should I call her tomorrow? Was this a one-time thing?*

Kissing Steph as an adult was different, and much better. It was slow, deep, and drowned out all the questions buzzing through his head. Because there was no room for thought or analysis. There was just her . . . Her clean shampoo scent, her taste, her warmth, the smoothness of her skin. How the pulse of her neck fluttered when he pressed his mouth there. The way she gasped when he nipped her ear. How she pressed against him, closing any space between their bodies. How her mouth claimed his, over and over, as if she, too, hadn't ever stopped thinking of him.

Nine

STEPH KNEW SHE SHOULD RELEASE Cal and slow things down. She hadn't kissed Nate like this, or anyone else for that matter. But she couldn't seem to get enough of Cal's mouth exploring hers. Everywhere his fingers touched, every place his lips traveled, had become like flames licking her skin.

"Cal," she whispered as his mouth made its way along her jaw and his hands threaded through her hair. "You upped your skills."

He smiled against her neck. "So did you."

She laughed. "I guess some things get better with age?"

"Mmm." His mouth found hers again, and she felt like she'd truly melted. She had no idea where his body ended and hers began.

She moved her hands along his shoulders, anchoring herself, enjoying the sensations that had invaded. She wasn't sure who kissed who first, but if there was to be a debate, it was probably her. She hadn't meant to kiss him and probably shouldn't have. He'd told her some really vulnerable things, and she'd jumped in with both feet—taking things to the next level.

A car's headlights flashed onto the street, and the sound

of its engine drawing closer brought Steph back to earth. She drew away from Cal's tempting kissing.

By the time the car neared, he had completely released her. Although he grasped her hand, which sent another wave of warmth through her. Maybe she hadn't been too impulsive. Maybe Cal wouldn't disappear for another ten years.

"I should get Pops to bed," she said in a fog-thick voice, "and you have a long drive ahead of you."

"Right," he rasped.

They started walking toward her house. Silence pulsed between them, and it would have been awkward if he hadn't kept her hand in his. "What are your plans next weekend?" he asked.

He couldn't have surprised her more. She looked up to find his gaze on hers. His expression might be shadowed by the trees that were currently blocking the moonlight, but his smile was warm.

"You're planning another trip to Everly Falls?" she asked, hope filtering through her.

"I don't know yet." Cal rubbed his thumb over her fingers, sending goose bumps skittering across her skin. "But I figure if you're going to kiss me like that, then you wouldn't be opposed to hanging out again."

Steph's heart skipped. "I wasn't planning to be so forward."

"Oh, I didn't mind."

His words buzzed through her, and she found herself grinning. Embarrassed and exhilarated all at once. "Maybe I will be free next weekend, then. What are you thinking?"

"I'll surprise you, how about that?"

"I like it," she said, wondering if she was jumping too fast into all of this. Her phone rang, and she pulled it out of her pocket, wondering if it was Pops.

Brandy's number flashed across the screen. She glanced at Cal, then answered. "Hey, how did it go with your mom?"

"Not well," Brandy said in a rush. "Can I possibly get Cal Conner's phone number? I'm wondering if he'll talk to my mom—she thinks we're ambushing her."

"Hang on a second," she said, then muted the call.

"I'll talk to her, no problem," Cal said. Clearly he'd heard Brandy's panicked voice.

Steph unmuted the call. "Hey, Brandy, he's right here. I'll hand him the phone." She gave it to Cal.

Brandy's tinny voice came through the phone, explaining to her mom that Cal was on the line.

Once they reached her front yard, she headed inside to check on her grandpa.

Pops turned to look at her when she entered. The baseball game was over, and some news program played. "Where's your boyfriend?"

She didn't even bother to correct him. "Cal's on the phone, but he'll be leaving soon. Let's turn off the TV and start shutting things down for the night."

"I'm not five years old," Pops grumbled. "I want to say goodbye to Cal. Wish him a safe drive home."

Well, she couldn't argue with that. So she settled on the couch and waited with him.

"He's a fine man," Pops said. "Very handy. Do you think he can come back next weekend? While you were both out on your walk, I thought of a few other things that need fixing around here. My old bones might break if I try."

Steph leaned forward and frowned. "Don't you dare ask him anything. I'll fix whatever's needed. I just need a little time."

He looked at her like she'd grown a second head. "I've heard that excuse before, and you're working too hard as it is. And those maintenance companies want to rob people blind."

"I'll have a free afternoon Wednesday, so you can give me your list, and I'll get started."

"That's when you fraternize with your friends—get all dolled up and go somewhere."

It was true, but she could skip a week, because there was no way she'd allow her grandpa to hit up Cal to do more house projects for them. "I'll see my friends later, so forget you ever thought of Cal helping out. He lives an hour away—"

"Who lives an hour away?" Cal said, his voice nearly making her jump.

She hadn't heard him come inside. Had he oiled the door hinges or something?

Pops grinned, and Steph didn't like that grin one bit.

"Oh, we were just talking about you behind your back." Pops chuckled. "My granddaughter here thinks she's Wonder Woman and can work a full-time job, take care of my sorry self, and do projects around the house to spec."

"Pops . . ." Steph said in as nonchalant a voice as possible, although she hoped he would take a hint.

Cal handed over the phone, and she wished they could have a private moment so she could get the update about Brandy and Lydia. But Pops rose out of his recliner.

"I'll walk you out, son," he said. "Need to stretch my legs before I miss my curfew."

Steph rose from the couch, too. She didn't really like the idea of him walking around in the dark, even if it was just to Cal's car.

"I'll be fine," Pops said before she could protest. "You can spy on us from the porch if you're so worried."

Apparently her grandpa was a mind reader.

"I'll watch him," Cal said.

She tried to read his eyes, his expression, and see any hints of what might have transpired with Lydia Kane. Well, she'd probably have to wait until he left and then call Brandy.

"Thanks for dinner," Cal said, his deep voice reaching across the room.

She nodded. "Thank you for all your help—it was above and beyond."

Pops had the front door open and was heading out.

Cal met him at the door, his eyes still on Steph. "It was no trouble," he said, right as Pops grasped his arm.

"I should probably hold on to you," Pops said. "These stairs can be tricky."

Cal threw a parting glance at Steph. One full of humor, and something else. Hope?

Hope for what? She was hoping that their tentative plans for next weekend would become a reality. And she hoped that Pops wouldn't make any requests that would make Cal feel obligated in other ways.

Steph stepped out onto the porch and watched the two men walk to the curb. Pops seemed intent on talking to Cal alone, and Steph could only guess what it meant. When the two men parted, she waved to Cal, who lifted his hand in goodbye.

By the time Pops carefully made it back to the house, Cal had driven off.

"What was that all about?" Steph asked him as she closed and locked the front door.

"Never you mind." Pops walked toward the hallway and disappeared, leaving her standing in the middle of the room.

She turned off the TV, then heard the water running in the bathroom. It seemed like Pops was taking his bedtime routine seriously tonight. She moved into the kitchen, where everything was cleaned up and put away—thanks to Cal's help.

After turning off the main lights, she heard Pops's bedroom door shut. Had he already gone to bed? Without telling her his sweet tooth was acting up, or that he wanted to catch *The Late Show*, or that he had some sort of mysterious malady that she needed to cure?

Steph paused by his bedroom door. She heard the creak of his mattress, and then a few seconds later, his light switched off. The only light coming through the space at the bottom of his door was the faint glow of the nightlight.

Huh.

She moved to her own bedroom, leaving the door ajar like she always did so she could hear if Pops got up in the middle of the night. She called Brandy. The phone rang a few times, then went to voice mail. So she texted her friend. *Checking in for an update. How did it go talking to Cal? I wasn't able to ask before he left.*

Steph climbed into bed and settled against her stacked pillows. She tugged one against her chest and let her eyes flutter shut. Kissing Cal had been . . . amazing. A week ago, she wouldn't have ever imagined that Cal would be at her house, fixing stuff, cooking dinner, treating Pops like gold, kissing her on a dark street, making her pulse race like she was training for the Olympics . . .

Her phone rang, and she opened her eyes and grabbed it. *Brandy.*

"Are you up reading some scary book?" Brandy teased.

"No . . . I have other things on my mind. How did it go with your mom?"

"Much better after talking to Cal." Brandy's voice sounded tired. "But my mom's still in shock, I think. She was really interested in Greg. Even though Cal explained that he didn't know the full story behind all those divorces, Mom agreed that they were too much of a red flag. Even if she could explain away the age differences in the women he'd married."

Relief buzzed through Steph. "I'm so glad she took the information seriously. Is she okay otherwise?"

"She deleted that dating app, if that's what you mean."

"Good idea, unless she's willing to have you or Everly help her filter through all the junk."

"Yeah . . . I don't think that's going to happen," Brandy said. "She does want to date, but both my sister and I told her we'd help her look up singles' activities and events where she could meet men more naturally—and safely. Everly said she's heard of a widows' group—and they do monthly activities in various towns."

"That sounds really interesting."

"Yeah, I thought so, too." Brandy sighed. "Mom has some wounds to nurse first, then maybe we can talk her into more."

"What about Greg? Did she end things with him already?"

"Oh yeah. Cal insisted on it. Said to text him a quick goodbye, then block his number. He said there was no reason to be cruel, but that it needed to completely end."

Steph found herself pleased with Cal all over again. Not that it was hard to do. He was checking quite a few boxes.

"So . . ." Brandy said in a brighter voice. "Cal was at your house? What was that all about?"

Steph had filled in her friends about their quick chat after the reunion—well, she made it sound a lot quicker than it was. Brandy was the only one who knew he was coming into town and that Steph had asked for his investigative help. "Well . . . I invited him for dinner, and it turned out he arrived quite early, while I was still at work, and ended up being Pops's personal maintenance man."

"What?" Brandy asked with a laugh.

Steph filled her in on the rest, except for the evening walk and the all-consuming kissing session. If Cal came out again next weekend, and things continued to progress, then it would be easy to catch up her girlfriends. But if things didn't align, then she wouldn't have to go through the whole "I'm a magnet for unavailable men" explanation again.

"Wow," Brandy said at length. "He fixed all that stuff? I'd be surprised if he ever returned to Everly Falls again."

"Right?" Steph sighed. "I think Pops is in love with him. He's like a new man around Cal."

"And you?" she asked. "Are you a new woman?"

"It would take a lot more than a few repairs and a report on Greg Makin to make me consider a guy like Cal Conner, no matter how good looking he is." *And more than one hot kiss.*

"Ooo. Sounds very promising to me."

"Time will tell," Steph said in the most mellow tone she could muster. "I'm not holding my breath for anyone anymore."

Even as she said the words, she knew that she'd already opened her heart to Cal. Maybe too much, too soon. She needed to guard herself more carefully. Because as amazing as Cal had been to her, to Pops, and about everything, some things were too good to be true. She'd learned that plenty over the past few years.

Ten

"I'VE EMAILED YOUR ATTORNEY ALL of the reports," Cal told his client Steve Ross.

"I don't know how to thank you," Steve said. "This is going to help my custody battle. I'm hoping to get my kids for the full summer next year. I've already lined up vacation days and talked to my boss about working remote while the kids are with me."

"That sounds excellent, and a judge would be pleased to hear it," Cal said. "I wish you all the luck."

After hanging up with Steve, he leaned back in his chair. Not all of his investigations had positive outcomes, but they did allow his clients to move forward in their lives, and not to be stuck in an impossible situation. If everything went well with Steve's case, his kids would benefit from spending more time with the parent who actually paid them attention.

Cal knew there were always two sides to every story, but Steve's ex-wife had made no secret of her vacations away from her kids while they were home alone.

He turned to his phone and pulled up the series of texts he'd exchanged with Steph that week. They were light, flirty even, and the most important part of it was that they had a date this afternoon to go hiking. Right after he helped her grandpa paint the back fence. This time, though, Steph knew about the work project. She wasn't too happy about it, but he assured her it would be a nice break for him.

And it would be.

Cal just had to wrap his head around how much he missed Steph. They'd only reconnected a short time ago, and yet . . . she was constantly on his mind. Maybe it was because of their pretty intense kissing session? He shouldn't have analyzed it, but he had—did she kiss all the men she dated with equal fervor? Or was something growing between them?

Maybe he was obsessing over her because she was from his past and he was still trying to heal some of those parts. Or maybe it was because he was older now, and ready to look commitment in the face . . . That was what had his pulse bouncing around right now.

He was thinking of Steph way beyond a couple of weekend dates, beyond flirting and kissing and reminiscing. When he thought of her, he sensed she might be the real deal. And for some reason, that didn't scare him off or worry him. It made him excited to see her again. But was he becoming too attached too fast?

She was a woman who wore her heart on her sleeve. Embraced life as it came. Doled out plenty of affection and attention to everyone she knew. Which was both awe-inspiring and intimidating. Maybe he was a project to her—maybe he always had been. There was chemistry between them, sure. No one could deny that. But maybe she wasn't one of those girls who wanted a serious relationship and was perfectly happy flitting from one man to the next.

Maybe he should cancel. Put off the painting project. Tell her he'd come another weekend. He'd been alone most of his life. And he knew he felt comfortable in that aloneness.

Just Add Friendship

Keeping things to himself was always easier. Not having to explain or report was what he preferred. Yet, he'd been able to talk to Steph easily. He'd told her way more than he'd planned, and he still wanted to share things with her.

If he canceled their Saturday, then he could let his emotions cool off, let reason return. He wanted to help with the project, but he knew he'd spend the day becoming more attached to her.

"Cancel it," he whispered to himself. But he knew he wouldn't. No, he knew he *couldn't*.

Cal stood from his office chair and walked into the main part of his town house. He'd already loaded paint supplies in his car. On the kitchen table sat his backpack for the hike and a change of clothing. He was currently wearing his oldest jeans and a faded T-shirt. Perfect for painting fences.

Ignoring his colliding thoughts, he picked up his stuff and headed out the door. In an hour, he'd be in Everly Falls, likely talking himself out of this more than once on the drive. He'd help paint the fence, then go from there. One hour at a time.

When he pulled up in front of Steph's house, his stomach was in knots. He was back to being a seventeen-year-old boy. How were they supposed to greet each other? Would their easy rapport continue in person after a week of texting?

He climbed out of his car, and as he was gathering the paint supplies he'd loaded into his trunk, he heard Steph.

"Hey, there."

He straightened, holding a couple of drip pans and brushes, and turned to see her walking down the driveway. She must have come from the side yard.

"Hey."

She continued walking straight toward him, her eyes

bluer than the sky, and a soft smile on her face. It was a warm fall day, and she wore old sneakers and a faded red knit dress. Was she going to paint in that? Her hair was pulled into a high ponytail, and she already had something white smudged on her cheek.

"Did you start already?"

She smiled. "I've been painting for hours, slowpoke."

He smiled back. "I'm early."

She laughed, and his heart soared. Then she closed the distance between them and wrapped her arms about him.

His hands were full, but he pulled her close anyway. He could get used to this hugging thing. His heart rate continued to climb as her hair brushed his neck, and her shampooed scent enveloped him.

"How are you?" she asked, drawing away, but keeping her arms looped about his neck.

"Much better now." Would it be tacky to kiss her in front of her whole neighborhood? It seemed she didn't have much trouble with it after dark.

Before he could lean in, she stepped out of his arms. "Let's go, Pops is waiting."

"Yes, ma'am."

She led the way around the house, and Cal told himself to relax. The hug had been nice, more than nice, but only told him that Steph was . . . friendly? Interested in him? More interested in him than she was in the other people in all those photos on social media?

He told his brain to stop overanalyzing, stop obsessing, to just enjoy the day. Enjoy the beautiful, vivacious woman who happened to be paying him all kinds of attention right now.

Well, right now, she was technically instructing him about how the painting would go.

Just Add Friendship

He figured there was more than one way to accomplish something, and he could do things her way.

"We're not starting with sanding," Pops said, cutting into Steph's instructions. "I spent all day prepping yesterday, and it's ready for painting."

Steph set her hands on her hips and faced her grandpa. "I don't know what you did all day yesterday, but nothing has been sanded."

He walked over to the card table set up in the yard and picked up a worn piece of sandpaper. "Here's the proof, missy."

Steph pressed her lips together.

Even Cal could see splinters poking out from the wooden fence. Maybe Pops had sanded, but it needed to be more thorough.

"How about I do a few touchups while you two start painting at one end?" Cal offered.

Pops scowled, but Steph clapped her hands together. "That's an excellent plan, don't you think, Pops?"

He didn't answer, unless a grumble counted. Cal decided not to ask if one of their neighbors had a sander. He picked up the seen-better-days sandpaper and set to work. Over the next hour, he went through every scrap of sandpaper, then had to make a run to the hardware store. Not only for sandpaper, but for another couple gallons of paint.

He picked up sandwiches at the deli along the way.

"Oh, you're a lifesaver, Cal," Pops said when he returned.

"I was planning on making us lunch," Steph said.

He couldn't quite read her tone. Was she annoyed? Who'd be annoyed with lunch—no matter where it came from?

"These are much better and faster," Pops said, taking a huge bite from his sandwich. He hadn't bothered to clean his hands, and paint flecks mixed with his food.

Cal looked over at Steph to find her inspecting the sandwich fixings, a slight frown on her face.

"Do you not like turkey? There's a ham one, too. You take whichever one you like."

She looked up at him. "Turkey's fine, unless you want it?"

"I'll eat anything."

Her expression softened. "Anything?"

"Except asparagus and broccoli. Oh, and I don't really like artichoke."

"Okay, I'll keep that in mind." Her expression sobered again. "You really didn't have to buy us lunch—and do our errands. How much was everything?"

Pops had moved away, the sandwich dangling from his mouth as he began to paint again, sitting on the plastic chair that Steph had instructed him to use.

"It wasn't much," Cal said, stepping toward her. "I'm sorry I didn't ask about the lunch plans, but I think I see what's going on here."

Her eyes flew to his. In their blue depths, he saw both curiosity and wariness.

"What are you talking about?"

"You've been doing everything for your grandpa for years," Cal said, lowering his voice. "And I know he's grateful, and I'm sure your parents are, too, but it's hard. No matter what you say or what you pretend to feel."

Steph lifted her chin. "I'm fine, Cal. It's no trouble. I live here rent-free, and it's the least I can do for my own grandpa."

"I understand." He reached for her hand. "It's okay for someone to help. I mean, you help other people all the time.

Just Add Friendship

Why are you so stubborn about allowing someone to help you?"

Her breath released, and she looked away from him. "It's not about that. I . . ." Finally, she looked at him again. "I want Pops to feel happy. He's lost so much, and his body isn't cooperating either."

"And no one else can help you with him?"

She bit her lip. "I like you, Cal, I really do, but you can't keep paying for stuff and not let me pay you back."

He wasn't sure what she meant. "You don't have to repay me. If I didn't want to be here, I wouldn't."

"You say that now." Her blue eyes met his straight on. "But that will change. People always want something in the end."

Cal tugged her hand and drew her farther away from Pops. "What are you talking about? Your friends? Your former boyfriends?"

She blinked, but didn't answer.

"Was it a man who said you owed him?"

Her eyes filled with tears then, and he felt like he'd been slammed in the chest with a barbell.

"I think my problem is that I always see the good in people, or try to see the good in them, and some people just aren't good."

Cal threaded their fingers together. "It can be hard to stomach, that's for sure. My job is literally to find out a person's misdeeds. That makes it hard to have faith in people sometimes."

Steph nodded.

"What happened, Bee?"

She wiped at her cheeks. "Now's not the time." She shrugged and gave him a smile that was far from convincing. "Thanks for being here. I'm sorry to melt down on you. I'm really bad at accepting another person's help, like you said."

She stepped back, but he kept ahold of her hand. "That's not a terrible fault."

Her smile turned watery.

"Come here." He pulled her into his arms. At this moment, he didn't care if Pops was only a few yards away. Maybe he'd notice, and maybe he wouldn't.

Steph seemed to melt against him, but her breathing was calm, and he hoped that meant the tears had passed.

"I'm not getting any younger," Pops said without turning.

Did he have eyes in the back of his head?

Steph pulled away; her mouth turned up in a smile. "Back to work, mister."

He leaned down and kissed her cheek.

Her smile grew, and she squeezed his arm and headed to the fence.

Cal watched her for a second, happy she seemed better, but not happy with whatever had made her mistrust help. Was it a former boyfriend? Or just an all-around jerk? Someone in her family?

Eleven

STEPH WASN'T SURE WHY SHE'D made such a big deal about Cal buying lunch. He was being a good sport helping out with the fence, and doing everything else. It was great of him, sure, but also made her feel like it was too much. Too good to be true. Cal popped back into her life after ten years, and suddenly they were in a relationship?

Well, nothing had been defined yet, but she liked him more with every minute she spent with him. And if his story was true—which she had no reason not to believe—he was available. Their connection to their past was certainly a strong bond, but they were both adults now, had lived a lot more life, and their flirtation wasn't harmless.

But she didn't want her heart to become involved so quickly, like it had with other men she'd dated.

Was this just her thing? Steph always became wrapped up in a guy too soon, too fast, and then things would crash and burn. So many times she'd let her hopes rise, and each and every time, they'd been dashed.

Cal was different. Right? He was certainly different than the usual guys she dated, but maybe the bad luck was on her. Did that mean their relationship was doomed?

She glanced over at him. He'd finished sanding and was now painting on the north part of the fence. His strokes were long, even, and covering territory faster than her and Pops put together. Cal's help would mean this project wouldn't take more than a day.

Her phone buzzed, but she ignored it. Probably the group text chatting about next week's plans. Her friends hadn't been happy she'd ditched them this past week, but it was the only way she could get the to-dos done that Pops had suddenly insisted on. Kind of ironic because in the past, he'd told her not to worry about things. It was like Cal had awakened something inside of him. A handyman urgency of some sort.

Ten minutes later, when her phone rang, Steph sighed and set down the paintbrush. She fished her phone out of her pocket with her cleanest hand.

"Hey, Brandy," she said.

"Didn't you see the texts from Julie's husband? She's in labor right now, and things aren't going well."

"What? What's wrong?" Steph hurried to the table and set her brush on the paint can lid. Julie's baby wasn't due for another three weeks.

"The baby's heart rate is slowing, so they might have to do a C-section," Brandy said. "Dave's beside himself. His mom is out of town, so he texted our group from Julie's phone. I'm already at the hospital, and Lori is on her way."

"I'll come, too," Steph said. Pops watched her from his chair, and Cal walked across the yard toward her. "Be there soon."

She pocketed her phone. "It's my friend Julie. She's in labor and things aren't going well." Emotion tightened her throat. "I—I need to go to the hospital."

"Do you want me to drive you?" Cal asked in a quiet, calm voice.

She drew in a breath and met his gaze. "No. I can drive. I just . . ." She waved a hand. "Sorry about all this."

"Go ahead," Pops said, conciliatory for a change. "We'll finish up here."

"Yes," Cal echoed. "Don't worry about the fence. Go support your friend."

Steph nodded, blinking against the stinging in her eyes. "Thanks," she whispered, because that was all she could get out.

She hardly remembered the drive, and when she pulled into a parking space at the hospital, she wasn't even sure how she got there. Jumping out of her car, she hurried to the entrance.

It didn't take long to find Brandy and Lori in the very blue lobby of the maternity ward. Brandy wore a baseball cap, her hair in a messy braid, and Lori's dark hair was pulled into a ponytail. Her two friends rose from their chairs as she hurried toward them.

"Where's Dave?" Steph asked. "How's Julie?"

"Dave went back there to sign paperwork," Brandy answered. "They're doing the C-section ASAP."

Both friends hugged her, and Steph felt her body sag. When she drew away, she asked, "So this will fix the issue? Julie and the baby will be all right?"

"That's what everyone is hoping for," Brandy said.

"What about Maren?" Steph asked. "Who's watching her?"

"Their neighbor, Mrs. Lovell."

She nodded and sank into a nearby chair. They all sat in silence for several long minutes. When Dave returned to the lobby, hollows darkened the area beneath his eyes.

"Dave." Steph stood to hug him. "Any updates?"

He released her and scrubbed a hand through his

reddish-blond hair. "She's been wheeled into the operating room. So all we can do now is wait."

The minutes ticked by, and they alternated between conversation and long moments of silence. A text came from Cal, and Steph replied with the update. Which wasn't really an update at all. *Still waiting to hear any news.*

Keep me posted, he wrote. *Fence is done, and everything is cleaned up. I can bring you and your friends some food.*

Even if she had a gourmet meal, Steph knew she couldn't eat a bite. *Thanks, but we're all fine. I don't think any of us are hungry.*

"Who's that?" Brandy asked, her eyes tired and puffy.

"Cal," she said in a quiet voice. "He came over this morning to help me and Pops paint the back fence."

Brandy's brows lifted at this, and Steph braced herself for a barrage of questions, when a nurse bustled into the lobby. She decided the woman's cheerful expression could only be good news.

"You have a son," she told Dave. "He's being checked over, but everything seems fine so far. And Julie is just waking up. They're both fighters."

Dave wiped at the tears falling on his cheeks. "Can I see her?"

"Of course."

He turned toward Steph and the others. "Thank you for coming. I'm sure she'll want to see you, too."

"You go ahead," Brandy said with a wave of her hand. "We can wait."

Steph leaned back in her chair, relief flowing through her. "Thank goodness. I hope that little guy will be fine." She texted Cal the update. Seconds later, her phone rang. She was surprised that he was calling her, so she walked out of the lobby and into the parking lot to answer it.

"Hello?"

"How are you?" Cal asked.

"Relieved. The nurse said Julie and her new baby will be fine."

"That's really great news," he said, his voice warm. "But how are *you*?"

"I'm good." She puffed out a breath and stopped by her car. "No one needs to worry about me—I'm not the one who had a C-section."

"But your friend did, and I wanted to make sure you're okay."

Steph didn't know why tears filled her eyes. "You're sweet, Cal, but I don't need any fussing over. How did the rest of the fence go?"

"We got it done in no time, probably faster because you weren't here distracting me."

"Funny." She sighed, leaning against her car. "Sorry I ran out on everything."

"Bee, you don't need to apologize for going to help your friends."

"Well, it's not exactly that," she said. "I don't think I'm up for the hike we planned. I don't want to abandon everyone, and I might be helping Dave with his toddler. She's with their neighbor, who's as old as the hills."

"That old, huh?" Cal asked, his tone amused.

"I feel bad that you came all the way to Everly Falls to do my chores."

Cal didn't laugh. "I was happy to do it, like I told you. So if you're done apologizing, text me what you and your friends want for dinner. I'm bringing food over. And if you don't text me your orders, you'll have to live with whatever I get."

"Cal—"

"It's no trouble, I promise."

She blinked against another round of tears. "I was really scared," she whispered.

"I know," he said softly. "Everything's going to be all right though. I talked to Rachel, and she's going to check in on your friend, too. Told me that the maternity staff there is excellent."

"You're making me cry," Steph said, her voice trembling.

"As long as they're good tears?"

"They are."

"Good." The smile was plain in his voice, and Steph really wished he were standing in front of her so she could hug him. "Don't forget to text me the food orders. I'm heading out in about fifteen minutes."

"Okay." After hanging up with Cal, she headed into the hospital. She knew her friends were about to have a lot more questions about him. She wouldn't be able to answer them, but that didn't matter. She was happy he wasn't leaving Everly Falls quite yet.

Julie was still groggy by the time Steph visited her hospital room, but she looked serene. Dave had parked himself by her bed.

"I'll watch Maren overnight for you," Steph offered. She didn't have to work tomorrow, and it would help her to keep busy instead of sitting around worrying.

Dave's frown appeared. "Are you sure? Maren is a handful."

"If Mrs. Lovell can manage her, then I can definitely manage her."

"Maren loves you, Steph," Julie said in a drowsy voice.

Steph squeezed her hand. "And I love her."

Dave nodded, eyes full of gratitude. "I'll write down a

list of her favorite foods and her bedtime routine. This means the world."

"No problem." Her phone buzzed with Cal's text saying that he'd arrived with food.

"Cal Conner is dropping off some food," she told Dave and Julie. "I can bring some to you?"

"Oh thanks, but I'm not hungry," Julie said.

"I'll come out a little later," Dave added.

So Steph headed to the lobby. There she found Cal surrounded by Brandy and Lori, who were acting more than curious, completely ignoring the bags of food while asking him a bunch of questions.

"Steph," Cal said the instant he spotted her. His face lit with that smile she loved. She marveled again at the changes in this man over the years.

"Hey, thanks for doing this."

"You're welcome." His brown eyes held hers, and she wished they were alone. As it was, Brandy and Lori seemed to be hanging on each word. "How's Julie and her baby?"

"Julie's doing great, and the nurse said the baby's oxygen and blood pressure are stable."

"That's good news."

"Yeah." She paused. "You want to stay and eat with us?"

He hesitated. "I have a couple of things I need to do."

"Right, and get back to Grandin eventually."

"Right." He looked over at Brandy and Lori, who were pretending to be busy getting their food arranged. "It was great to see you ladies again. Have a good night."

"Great to see you, too, Cal," Brandy said in a singsong voice.

"Drive safe," Lori added.

"I'll walk you out." Steph didn't want their goodbye to be more awkward than the situation already was.

She and Cal walked out of the hospital. Most of the cars in the general parking lot were gone, and the sunset bathed everything in an orange glow.

"Thanks again, Cal." Steph glanced at his handsome profile. He'd cleaned up, but there were paint specks all over his shirt and jeans. She caught herself admiring his easy walk and his broad shoulders. "My friends aren't going to forget this anytime soon."

One side of his mouth lifted as his gaze connected with hers. "It's kind of crazy to see them again—the more things change, the more they stay the same."

"Which is a good thing, in my opinion."

Cal's steps slowed as they reached his car. "I agree."

Why was her pulse racing? Just because Cal had brought them food, and he was all male in his fitted T-shirt and well-worn jeans? "I'd offer to pay you back, but I know you'd say no."

His gaze searched hers, and she saw the question there. "You're right about that." He grasped her hand, tentatively, as if he wasn't sure how she'd react.

She looked down at his hand linked with her fingers. His was more olive than her pale, freckled skin.

"You're kind of a lot, Cal," Steph said. "No offense."

His brows rose, but he leaned against his car, and drew her closer. "I'm not offended, but what do you mean?"

"I mean . . ." She liked the warmth and sturdiness of his hand encasing hers. "What are we doing here? We haven't communicated in ten years, and now in just one week, you're doing chores at my house and bringing me and my friends food."

Cal said nothing, his gaze remaining steady.

"I'm grateful for all your help, but I don't understand it."

He didn't seem fazed. "I like you, Bee. It's as simple as that."

She studied his face and saw nothing but sincerity there. "I like you, too, Cal. Obviously."

He smiled.

"But I'm also worried."

One of his brows lifted. "About what?"

"That you're too good to be true..."

He straightened from the car and released her hand, a frown appearing. "You mean like Greg Makin?"

"No." Steph's stomach twisted. "Not like a guy who's trying to set up another person. I just wondered why you're being so... awesome."

Cal stared at her for a moment. "I'm far from awesome, Steph. But if I can help out someone I care about, I will. It's honestly been a long time since I've been able to or even *cared* to."

She went silent at that.

"I don't want to scare you off or anything, so maybe you're right," he said carefully. "Maybe I shouldn't be saying this now, but I want you to know that I like you. A lot. And I also know I can be a bit persistent in things—it serves my line of work well—but I also don't want to overwhelm you."

"I'm not overwhelmed," she said quickly, then sighed. "Okay, maybe just a little."

His mouth quirked, and he nodded. "Fair enough. How about we keep the ball in your court for now. You decide how much or how little you want from me."

"Okay," she said, not exactly sure what she was agreeing to. But he was kind of distracting with his hunky good looks. Also, how did this man smell good after working most of the day in her yard? "Did you shower?"

His brows tugged together. "No. But I probably need to."

"You're fine, I just . . . you smell good."

"Like paint?"

She moved closer and rested her hand at his waist. The cotton of his shirt was soft beneath her fingers. "Like . . . a man who worked all day in my yard."

He chuckled. "That doesn't sound pleasant. And you touching me is not helping me leave the ball in your court."

She moved her other hand to his waist and curled her fingers into his shirt. "Why not?"

His eyes darkened. "Because I want to kiss you right now."

"What's stopping you?"

His hands cradled her face, the warmth of his fingers sending goose bumps along her skin. "I don't want to be too forward," he whispered.

She moved her hands around to his back, drawing him flush against her. "I approve of goodbye kisses."

"In that case—" He didn't finish his sentence because he pressed his mouth against hers.

She moved up on her toes to get closer, to kiss him deeper. Fire filled her veins as he explored her mouth. It was a long moment before she breathed again. "Are all of our kisses going to be public?"

His voice rasped with his answer. "I should hope not."

She laughed, and then she kissed him again, her arms anchored around him. She was probably sending him mixed messages, but right now, she didn't care.

Twelve

When Cal's phone rang Sunday afternoon, tension rolled off his shoulders. Steph was calling him. He hoped everything was okay with her friend, but mostly he wanted to hear from her. Their conversation in the parking lot the day before had raised a few warning flags, but then they'd kissed, and then . . . he didn't know what then. He liked her, and he knew she liked him. But relationship territory could be rocky.

"Hey there," he answered. There was no use pretending he didn't know she was calling.

"Hi." Her voice was low, soft.

When she didn't say anything immediately, he asked, "How's the babysitting?"

"Maren just went down for a nap," Steph said. "I thought she'd never crash, and I'm exhausted."

"So you called me?" He couldn't keep the smile off his face. He leaned back in his office chair and propped a leg up on a box.

"Yeah . . . I guess I did."

He imagined he heard the smile in her voice, too, and hoped he wasn't wrong.

"I was thinking about all your help, and—"

"Please don't thank me again, Bee," he cut in. "I already told you that I was happy to help."

"I know," she said on a sigh. "You're . . . so different than other guys I've dated."

This both alerted him and made him pleased. Very pleased. "Are we dating?"

"Uh, that's not what I meant."

He chuckled. "Too late to take it back. Besides, I think kissing in public means we're dating."

"Cal . . ."

When she didn't continue, he said, "Sorry, I forgot the ball's in your court."

"It is . . ."

This time, when she paused, he waited for her to finish.

"Look, I wanted to ask if you'd be interested in coming to a barbecue with me next weekend at Ian's cabin. He's the one dating Brandy."

Cal was so stunned, he didn't answer at first.

"You can say no if you want."

"No—I mean, yes," he said. "I'd love to."

"I thought it would be fun for you to see some of our old high school friends, and you know, hang out with me while not painting the fence or fixing a faucet at my house."

Cal was more than pleased to be invited, but he had to clear a couple of things up. "I didn't have friends at that high school, Bee, except for you. But I'd love to hang out with *your* friends. Although, I have to ask, is this a date?"

"Maybe?"

Cal shifted forward in his chair. "Maybe? What does that mean?"

"It means that it's what you want it to be. It could be hanging out with a group of people, or it could be going on a date with me where we end up hanging out with a group of people."

He laughed. "And we arrive and leave together?"

"Yeah."

"Will there be any public kissing?"

Steph let out a small gasp. "Definitely not."

He was grinning. "My answer is yes to going, and yes, I'm considering this a date, but there is one problem."

"What's that?" she asked, her voice turning wary.

"Next weekend is a long time to wait to see you again." It was okay for him to state his opinion, but still leave things up to her, right? "I miss you, that's all. But don't let it go to your head because the ball's still in your court."

"Next weekend does seem like a long time, but I think it's good for me."

Now this intrigued him. "Why's that?"

"Just because . . ." Her tone turned reluctant. "I have a bad track record of relationships moving too fast, then crashing and burning. Well, at least for me—the guy always seems to move on just fine."

Cal wasn't sure what to make of her statement. "How many boyfriends have you had?"

"I don't know the answer to that because I think the definition varies depending on who you ask."

"What's your definition of a boyfriend?" Cal rose from his desk and crossed to the window overlooking the street. Orange and red leaves dangled from the trees, swaying in the breeze. Otherwise things looked pretty deserted, since not many people were out and about on this lazy Sunday afternoon.

"When two people are mutually exclusive and like each other the same amount."

"That sounds about right," Cal said. "So how many?"

"I still don't know because I think I've liked each guy I've dated more than he's liked me."

He found this hard to believe—but it seemed to be what she believed. "So every guy you've dated has dumped you?"

"Yeah, pretty much."

He wanted specifics, because how could Steph be the only one investing in a relationship with a man? "What's an example?"

"Well . . . the last man I dated, it lasted three weeks," Steph said.

They were coming up on three weeks between them, if he was counting.

"Nate had told me about his ex-girlfriend," she continued, "and she sounded like a complete nightmare. But to my surprise, one phone call from her sent him running back."

"That's nothing against you, though," Cal said, moving away from the window and heading out of his office toward the kitchen. "He was already in love with someone else."

"Yeah, maybe," she said with a sigh. "But that doesn't explain John Parker bringing me flowers every day for weeks, then he completely ghosts me. When I ran into his sister a few days later, she said he'd taken a job in another city. No word to me. Which only tells me he didn't like me enough to do anything long distance."

Before Cal could reply that John Parker sounded like a rotten guy, she said, "And then there was Drew Larson, who invited me to holiday parties with his family, and the day after Christmas, he told me we couldn't see each other again because his mom didn't like me."

"What?" Cal paused as he was about to open his fridge.

"Yeah, and then Jeremy Baker told me I was fun, but too small town for his future."

Just Add Friendship

"Steph—"

"Not to mention Lyle Gibson, who I thought adored everything about me, only to find out that he was hoping I'd go part-time at the salon to help with his two kids. He wasn't impressed that I wasn't a natural instant-mommy. I mean, I wasn't opposed to the stepmom thing, but I wasn't going to switch to part-time when we didn't even have marriage plans."

"It's not you," Cal said, but Steph continued with her stories, ignoring his comment. He grabbed a water bottle out of the fridge.

"John Anders said my religion was a deal breaker."

Cal twisted the cap off the bottle. "What's your religion?"

"I don't have one. I mean do I think there's a God? Yes. But do I go to church outside of weddings? No."

"Steph, it's not you."

"And Henry Silva, well, he wasn't about to give up his wife for me."

Cal sputtered the water he'd just swallowed down. "What?"

Her laugh sounded hollow. "Don't worry, I stopped seeing him once he *told* me he was married. The jerk. But then there was Chris Monson, who asked me to change over his laundry when he was going to be late for our date."

Cal set down the water bottle on the counter and laughed.

"It's not a joke, it's true," Steph said.

"I'm sure it's true," he said. "Bee, you have to know that none of those things are your fault. All of those guys were idiots."

"How can that be true, though? Julie has a perfectly great husband. Brandy is dating an amazing guy. Everly is engaged to like a renaissance man. Yet every relationship I've had turned into unlivable complications. That tells me it *is* me. Or maybe I've been cursed?"

"Curses aren't real, but you are, Steph," he said. "You're the real deal, and those men missed out, because they were jerks."

"I didn't tell you all that stuff for your pity."

Cal rubbed the back of his neck. "I don't pity you. I admire you. And frankly, I'm glad none of those quote-unquote boyfriends stuck around."

Her voice was much quieter when she asked, "You are?"

"I am." He'd never been more sure of anything in his life. Steph still being single was the best news he'd probably ever had. He hadn't exactly realized it until this very moment. Hearing about the men who'd hurt her over and over again only made Cal feel more protective of her.

"What are you doing tonight?" he asked.

"Tonight?" The surprise was plain in her voice. "Babysitting. I told Dave I'd watch Maren one more night so he can stay with Julie in the hospital."

"Want some company?"

Steph laughed, then sobered. "Are you serious? What do you know about kids?"

"Not much, but I want to see you. I could bring dinner—what does she like to eat?"

"That's the million-dollar question for a three-year-old."

"So I'll bring some choices."

"Cal," she said. "I shouldn't have dumped so much on you—it wasn't meant to tell you that you have to be the hero."

"I'm not going to take offense to that, because I don't think you need rescuing," he said. "Or a hero. In fact, this is a selfish request since I want to spend time with you."

"We saw each other yesterday, plus I have Maren."

"Kids seem to like me. Just ask my neighbor."

"Sounds like a story I need to hear," Steph mused.

"Is that a yes? If I show up on Julie and Dave's doorstep in a couple of hours, you'll open the door?"

"Maybe? I mean, I just told you that not seeing you for a week might be a good thing—for me. You know, so I don't become too attached."

"That doesn't sound like an issue to me."

Steph laughed. "I can't believe I'm saying this, but yes, I'll open the door for you."

Everything warmed inside of him, and he'd have to talk himself out of not breaking speed limits. "Great. I have a couple of things to finish up, then I'll head out. Text me the address."

"Okay, see you soon." He felt gratified when he heard the smile in her reply.

Cal didn't have things to finish up. Well, he always had work he could do, and some weekends were busier than weekdays. But his current client was a law firm, and it was still in the process of sending him the information he'd requested. So that wouldn't likely come in today. Soon, though, he'd be following their client who was suspected of insurance fraud. That might mean he'd have to go dark for a few days, and he hoped it would be wrapped up by next weekend.

He'd worry about all that later. Right now, he had a woman to see.

Thirteen

INSTEAD OF READING OR TAKING a short nap, though she really was tired from a night of getting up several times with a three-year-old, Steph cleaned up the main parts of Julie's house. It wasn't exactly dirty, just normal toddler messy.

She had been planning on doing it anyway so that Julie and Dave could come home to a clean and organized house. But now that Cal was on his way, Steph felt a lot more motivated.

She had texted Julie first to make sure it was all right that Cal visited.

Julie was fine with it, and as Steph straightened up, she had a strange sense of surrealness come over her. Like she was straightening up during her own daughter's nap while waiting for her husband to come home. She shook the invading thoughts away. As far as she knew, Cal would turn out too good to be true. She just hadn't found his flaws yet.

A screech sounded from the other room. "Mommy!"

Maren was awake, and it was always in a panic. She didn't wake up happy.

Steph hurried to the toddler's bedroom and found her standing on top of her bed, trying to tug her shirt off.

"Hey, Maren, it's me, Steph, remember?" She crossed the floor. "Mommy's at the hospital with your baby brother."

Maren's wide green eyes surveyed Steph. Her hair had come out of its mini-ponytail and snarled about her head. "Where's my baby brother?"

"With your mommy." Steph reached the bed and held out her hand. "Do you have to go potty?"

She gave a solemn nod. Julie had told her that Maren would try to take off all her clothing when she had to use the bathroom.

"You can leave your shirt on," Steph said. "I'll help you with the rest in the bathroom."

Maren looked undecided, but Steph gently grasped her hand. "Come on, I'll help you get down. Do you want a treat after?"

Her green eyes brightened. "Treat?"

"Yep, you'll get to choose a treat."

"I want the Cinder-wella one."

"Okay." Steph helped her off the bed. Once they finished in the bathroom, and Maren was fully dressed, they got her treat.

But five minutes later, her eyes welled as she asked for her mommy again. Steph tried to distract her by saying, "Let's color a picture for your mom, okay?"

Ten minutes later, Maren asked for her mom again.

"How about we make cookies for your mom?"

"Big ones?"

Steph wasn't sure what she was committing to, but she said, "Yeah, big ones. How big is that?"

Maren shrugged, then dragged a chair over to the pantry.

Okay, so maybe she had done this with her mom, and it would be a fun activity for longer than just a few minutes.

Assembling the ingredients was a bit of a feat because Maren wanted to do everything "by myself," and Steph was cleaning up more spills than what actually made it into the bowl.

But at least the three-year-old wasn't whining for her mom anymore. So what if Steph ended up with a little more laundry once the cookies were finished?

"Can you help me roll the cookies into a ball?" she asked, showing Maren how she scooped about a spoonful and rolled it between her hands.

Maren stared at her with delight. Then she plunged her small hands into the bowl of dough.

"Not quite that much," Steph said as Maren drew out about half the dough, oozing between her fingers. Several dollops plopped onto the floor.

"Oh, whoops." She guided Maren's hands back over the bowl. "Just leave the dough in there, I'll get it out."

She turned to grab a paper towel to pick up the fallen dough, but before she could do any cleanup, Maren wailed, "I want to do it!"

"You can still do it," Steph said in the sweetest tone she could muster. "I need to show you how much—"

"No," she cried, flinging her hands, which only made more dough fly around.

One piece landed square on Steph's forehead. She released a slow breath. The sooner she got Maren out of the firing range of cookie dough, the better.

"Can you help me turn on the oven?"

"It's hot!" Maren wailed.

Steph's stomach tightened as the little girl dissolved into tears. She wasn't tired—she'd already taken a nap. So it must be missing her mom and the change of routine.

While Maren cried, her arms cradling her head on the

table, sounding like her heart had broken into a million pieces, Steph moved the bowl onto the counter out of reach. Then she wet a few paper towels and cleaned off Maren's hands, then began to wipe up the mess.

Who knew that a three-year-old could cry so loud for so long?

"Maren, sweetie?" Steph laid a hand on the small girl's heaving shoulder. "Should we go for a walk? Look at the trees and find some bugs?"

"I hate bugs!" she wailed.

Steph knew that wasn't true, but it seemed that emergency measures were needed. If she were a mother, maybe she'd know the magic trick of soothing a toddler, but Steph wasn't, and she could only think of one thing. It might be breaking a tiny rule on the list that Dave had given her about limiting screen time. She'd already taken Maren on a long walk earlier that day to visit Pops and check on him.

"Should we watch your pony movie?" Steph asked.

Just then, the front doorbell rang.

"It's Mommy!" Maren screeched, nearly falling off her chair in her haste to go answer the door.

Steph hurried after her. "You know only adults can answer the door."

"Mommy!" Maren said, tugging on the door handle, which wouldn't budge.

Steph peeked through the peephole. Her breath nearly left her. Cal was here . . . Had he heard the crying and all the commotion? Well, there was no turning back the clock now, and there was no telling Maren it wasn't her mom on the other side of the door. She'd just have to see for herself.

Steph unlocked the door and pulled it open as Maren wriggled past her. Then stopped in her tracks.

"You're not my mommy!" she declared, tears still wet on her reddened cheeks.

Credit went to Cal for not staring at the little girl in shock. He glanced at Steph with a raised brown, then he crouched to Maren's level. "My name is Calvin. What's your name?"

Calvin? Had Steph known that? She wanted to laugh or maybe cry with relief.

Maren scrunched up her blotchy face. "You're a stranger."

Cal nodded, resting his forearms on his knees. He wore dark jeans with a button-down shirt and dark jacket. "I'm Steph's friend. I brought over some dinner. Are you hungry?"

Maren's gaze was steady as she considered all that he'd said. "I had a Cinder-wella treat."

Cal looked suitably impressed. "You must have been a good girl."

Maren set a tiny fist on her tiny hip. "I went potty."

The edge of his mouth lifted. "Oh wow, you're a big girl, too. How old are you? Five?"

Maren giggled. "No, dummy, I'm three." She held up three adorable fingers.

"We don't use the word *dummy*, Maren." Steph had heard Julie correct her daughter's language many times, so she felt obligated now.

"Ryan says dummy." Maren looked up at Steph, her stubbornness returning.

"Ryan's not supposed to say it either," Steph said, not really wanting to argue with a three-year-old. "How about we show *Calvin* the picture you made for your mom?"

Cal straightened at that, a smirk on his face.

"Okay." Maren grasped Cal's hand and tugged him through the house.

Apparently he was no longer a stranger—an even better reason for a child not answering the front door.

"Calvin?" Steph whispered as he passed by her.

"Never came up," he said with a smirk. "Hang on," he told the precocious Maren. "Let me set these sacks on the table."

"What did you bring?" Maren asked, distracted from her original mission. She scrambled up on the chair and propped her elbows on the table.

"Well . . ." Cal made a great ceremony of opening the first bag and pulling out a circular container. "This is tomato soup."

Frown lines appeared on Maren's forehead. "I don't like tomatoes."

"Then good thing I also brought chicken noodle soup." Cal pulled out another container.

Maren's expression eased.

"There's also bread. Do you like to dip bread into soup?"

She brightened. "I can dip bread!"

"Great," Cal said with a chuckle. "Before we dip the bread, we need to see what else I brought."

He pulled out a couple of salads, a cup of fruit, and three different kinds of cookies. Maren was especially interested in the cookies.

Steph could kiss Cal right now. "We'll have the cookies after dinner."

Maren's pout returned.

"Steph is right," he said, his amused gaze flashing to her. "We have to eat dinner first."

"Okay." Maren seemed to idolize Cal. "I'll get the bowls!" She scooted off her chair and pushed it across the floor to the counter.

"Well." Steph nudged Cal's shoulder. "You have a fan."

He grinned, stirring up all kinds of butterflies in her stomach. "She's cute."

"I think the feeling is mutual." She gave him an approving smile. The last couple of times Steph had been around Cal, he'd been dressed down, doing a bunch of labor. But his button-down shirt was a very nice look on him. She decided she liked all of his looks, and especially whatever subtle cologne he wore. She was pretty sure it wasn't aftershave because the dark scruff on his face told her that he hadn't shaved that morning. She found herself wondering if it was soft or bristly.

He stepped close to her. "What's in your hair?"

"What's not in my hair?"

He plucked out a clump of cookie dough.

"Oh, we were making cookies."

Cal glanced about the kitchen. "Well, that's an understatement."

Maren was making a move to climb up on the counter, and Steph hurried over to her. "Here, I'll hand you the bowls, and you can take them to Cal."

Miraculously, she didn't protest.

Within a few minutes, they were all seated at the table, eating dinner as Maren peppered Cal with questions, such as: *Where do you live? How old are you? Do you like horses? How fast can you run?*

He answered each one, and Steph tried not to laugh. Maren hadn't even asked her those questions, and by the look in the little girl's eyes, she had a mini-crush on Cal. Steph sighed inwardly. She might, too.

After they finished dinner, Maren promptly ate her cookie, then said that she was ready for her mom to come home.

"I thought your charm would last a lot longer," Steph told Cal after they got her distracted again by helping her get the blocks out and build towers.

"Can we take her to see her mom?" he asked quietly.

"Um, maybe? I wasn't sure if I could manage tearing her away from her parents and taking her home sobbing . . . but maybe if you're with me?"

"I'll come with you."

"Okay, let me text Julie and see what she thinks." She grabbed her phone and texted Julie about Maren's new attachment and repeated requests to see her mommy. A few minutes later, Julie replied that she'd be thrilled if Steph could bring Maren and Cal to the hospital.

Cal can wait in the lobby, Steph clarified. *He doesn't want to intrude.*

He's already in my house, so bring him, too, Julie texted.

Funny. All right. We'll be there in about half an hour.

Steph had grossly underestimated the chore of getting Maren ready to visit the hospital, what with all the negotiating of what she'd wear and what she wanted to bring—not to mention that Steph didn't have a booster seat in her car.

"Your mom said you can ride in my car this one time without your booster seat." It was a complication that Steph had forgotten to bring up with Julie—so she was going on an assumption here. Otherwise, she'd have to ask Dave to drive back home. Would that defeat the purpose in helping with Maren?

But Maren stood her ground, arms folded, legs in a wide stance as she stood outside of Julie's car.

"Do you have any friends on this street?" Cal asked Maren.

"Ryan." She pointed a stubby finger to the house across the street. "He's four."

Ah, the kid who said *dummy* on the regular. Steph met Cal's gaze.

"Maybe we can borrow his booster seat?" she suggested, wondering if Maren would go for it.

"Okay," the little girl said.

The answer was so simple that Steph wasn't prepared. "Okay?"

"Okay."

Steph realized then that if she were ever a real parent, she'd be the biggest pushover ever. Because Maren's beaming face made her heart feel like it had grown twice its size.

"Well, then, let's go over and ask Ryan's mother if we can borrow his booster seat."

"Okay," Maren said again, slipping her small, soft hand in Steph's. Next, she grabbed Cal's hand so that the three of them walked across the street together.

"Good plan," Steph said to him.

He threw her a wink, and she was pretty sure she was now totally, one hundred percent attached to the man. *Easy, Steph,* she scolded herself.

Fourteen

Needless to say, Cal was impressed. He could tell Steph was worn out and wrung out by Julie's mini-me. Maren was certainly adorable, but mostly precocious. He was definitely glad he'd made the drive to help out a little—mainly, of course, to see Steph. But it had been fun to play babysitter for a bit, although now . . . he was in a bit of conundrum.

Steph was sound asleep next to him on the couch. Her head had lolled against his shoulder, then stayed there. She'd tucked her legs up at one point, and she was fully leaning against him.

To top it off, on his other side, Maren was snuggled against him with her blanket, three teddy bears, two dolls, and a bright yellow toy dump truck, while another episode of *My Little Pony* played on the television.

Cal wasn't even sure which movie app was on the screen, or how it continued through the episodes with no prompt from a remote control. And who knew what time it was because his cell sat face down on the coffee table, currently out of reach.

Cal turned his head to gauge if Maren was asleep, too. She hadn't made a peep for a while. Sure enough, her eyes were closed, her mouth slightly parted, and her breathing even.

Should he carry her to bed? Would that wake her? It would definitely wake Steph. Should he stay put? Let everyone sleep? It wasn't that he minded sitting on the couch for a while longer, but he didn't know how much more he could stand of watching cartoon ponies, or how Pinkie Pie found a way to make a copy of herself. The pony was very excited to spend time with her friends all at the same time and not have to choose between them.

The episode ended, and another began right away.

Then Steph's phone began to ring on the coffee table.

She straightened immediately, looked at him with surprise as if she'd forgotten why he was here, then she reached for her phone. Seeing who the caller was, she answered, moving away from the couch.

"Hi, Pops. Everything okay?" Pause. "It's in the laundry room." Another pause. "On the first shelf. I'll be home in the morning if you can wait . . . All right. Good night."

Steph pocketed her phone, then turned to Cal.

She looked adorably rumpled, hair tumbling about her shoulders, her V-neck shirt wrinkled, and her mascara smudged—makeup she didn't really need, in his opinion.

"I fell asleep on you."

Cal wasn't sure if it was a question. "You did." He nodded his head toward Maren. "Should we move her?"

Steph bit her lip. "Yeah, I mean, she can't sleep out here unless I do, too. Let me help extract her."

Together, they moved Maren enough so that Cal could stand. He switched off the infernal pony show, then lifted the child into his arms. "Lead the way."

Thankfully, Maren slept through the transfer, and once they made it back to the living room without incident, Cal was surprised to see that it was almost ten o'clock. "I should go," he said, although reluctantly. He'd love to stay longer, especially with a little peace and quiet from the ponies.

But he could see the exhaustion in Steph's eyes. And tomorrow she'd be working after Dave and Julie returned home.

She checked the time on her phone. "Oh wow, it's late. Sorry about falling asleep on you."

He only smiled. "It's fine. Gave me a lot of reflection time."

"About what?" The alarm on her face made him backtrack quickly.

"Wondering what would ever possess a person to stay awake during *My Little Pony*."

"Funny." Steph's expression had cleared, and he was happy about that. "Thanks so much, Cal. For your help tonight. Maren was about to fire me."

She was standing too far from him, near the door in fact. Was that on purpose?

"It was definitely entertaining," he said. "And I'm pretty sure your friend Julie is going to have her hands full."

"Yeah," Steph said with a smile. "She's a pro, though."

Cal nodded and grabbed his jacket from the back of the recliner. Then he moved toward Steph where she waited by the door. He paused . . . she paused. He wasn't sure why there was a hesitation between them right now. Maybe she just really wanted to have him leave so she could crash in bed.

"See you on the weekend?" he asked.

"Yep."

Another pause.

He reached for the doorknob, then before he could open the door, she stepped close and wrapped her arms about him.

Relief flowed through him, and he pulled her close.

"Drive safe," she murmured.

Could she feel the thumping of his heart? "I will. You have a good week at work."

"You too." She stepped away, and there was still something in her eyes that he couldn't read, couldn't define.

He wanted to pull her close again, and kiss her, and tell her things like how he was already missing her. But her eyes were too bright, her posture too erect.

"Good night, Bee."

As he drove away from the neighborhood, he realized he hadn't told her about his next few days of likely no contact. When he followed someone, he cut off all contact from other things in his life. It was why he didn't have a dog or cat or any plants to water. He never knew if a job would be a day or four days, or even longer.

He'd text her when he got home and let her know.

Then he could only hope that Steph would know he wasn't ghosting her, no matter how awkward their goodbye had been.

The following morning, Steph hadn't replied to the text he'd sent after he returned home. He assumed she'd gone to bed, and then this morning would be filled with the busyness of turning Maren over to her parents, and then going to work herself. She probably had a lot of catch-up to do as well after being away from Pops most of the weekend.

Cal told himself not to worry about her silence too much, but he worried anyway.

For the next three days, he lived out of a room in the hotel where the person he was profiling was staying. He was able to document the movements of the man suspected of insurance fraud, and his many meetings in the hotel lobby with elderly people who were led to believe they could take out life insurance at a high return when no other insurance company offered that. The man was quite blatant, in fact, taking large annual fees in the form of checks from his clients, then later in the afternoon heading to a bank to deposit them. It was all old-school and made it that much easier to track. For years, this man had been conning elderly people out of their money. Not one of their death benefits had been distributed—the insurance man claiming that their policy had expired or hadn't been paid in full.

On Cal's third day, he had more than enough evidence to turn over to the law firm, but he decided to stick around a little while longer and thwart the man's appointments. So he stood outside the hotel, out of sight from the lobby windows, and intercepted every elderly person he encountered. He'd ask them if they were meeting with a life insurance broker, and if they were, he'd break the news to them.

Most of them were shocked, but receptive. One older man blustered and accused Cal of trying to drum up his own business. Then the man headed into the hotel. It was time for Cal to leave.

A couple of hours later, he'd arrived home, and still seeing no reply from Steph, the worry he'd talked himself out of feeling returned in full force. She was likely at the salon right now, but he sat at his desk and called her anyway. After a few rings, his call went to voice mail. Well, at least she wasn't screening him, right?

"Hey, Bee," he said. "You're probably working. I wanted to check on you. See how you're doing. How's Julie's baby? How's Pops?" Too many questions. "Anyway, call me when you have a minute."

Surely a phone call would deserve a response. It was easy for a text to get lost in the shuffle. But for this many days? Wouldn't she reach out to him on her own, even if she hadn't acknowledged his earlier text? He hadn't imagined all the time they'd spent together—the fun, the flirting, the kissing.

And she'd invited him to the barbecue with her friends. Was that still on? Or more specifically, was he still invited?

There was nothing more he could do . . . except wait.

So he'd stay busy. While he'd been gone, plenty of work had come in.

When someone knocked at the door, he flinched. He'd been buried so deep in his work that he'd lost track of time, and apparently the sun was setting.

Cal stood, feeling stiff, and automatically checked his phone. Nothing from Steph. Maybe she'd come to Grandin? She didn't know his address, though, so there was no hope she was the one knocking on his door.

A quick glance through the peephole told him it was his neighbor. Diane.

He opened the door, and Diane smiled at him, although it was a bit harried. Her curly dark hair was tamed by a headband. Two kids clung to her legs, but the second they saw him, they launched themselves toward him.

"Hey, there," Cal said with a surprised laugh. Jeff and Jan were twin four-year-olds. "What's going on?" he asked Diane.

"Mr. Cal! Where are your glasses?" Jeff asked.

Was the kid talking about his sunglasses?

"Roger got held up at work," Diane said, "and I'm going to be late for my shift. Normally it wouldn't be a big deal, but tonight's inventory at the craft store. So no one can be late or miss, or we'll be fired."

"He doesn't wear glasses, dummy," Jan said.

"Mom, she called me dummy," Jeff complained.

"No one should call anyone dummy," Diane said, then looked back to Cal with an apologetic expression.

"So you need me to watch them until Roger gets home?" he asked.

"Do you know what a baby deer is called?" Jan asked him.

"A fawn?"

She beamed.

"If you could watch them, that would be a lifesaver," Diane said. "I know you just got back in town."

Cal didn't bother asking how she knew because Diane was one of those neighbors who knew what everyone in the complex was doing.

"How long do you think Roger will be?" he asked.

"He said an hour or two."

Roger worked for the fire department, so now Cal was wondering if there was a fire somewhere in the town, or other emergency. "That's fine."

He stepped outside and shut his door. He didn't really need anything, except his phone, and that was in his pocket. Everything the twins needed would be at their place.

"Thanks so much, Cal," Diane said, her tone warm. "You don't know what this means."

He could guess, and that was good enough.

"I owe you dinner—just let me know when you want to collect payment."

"It's a deal." Cal smiled and reined in the two kids by grabbing a hand each. Diane was a great cook, so it was a fair trade.

Fifteen

"HE'S TOO GOOD TO BE true," Steph told Brandy over the phone. She'd called to discuss the barbecue, but they'd ended up discussing Cal Conner instead.

"Is that possible?" Brandy asked. "Maybe you're just in love and wearing rose-colored glasses. Everyone has flaws—only his aren't bugging you."

"He *doesn't* have flaws." Steph had a client in about twenty minutes. In fact, it was Lydia, so Steph answered Brandy's call thinking it might be about her mom. "That's my whole point."

"What about all the tragedy he's been through? He was homeless, then estranged from his dad . . ."

"He's turned all those things into strengths," Steph complained as she sorted the shipment of hair product that had arrived earlier in the day.

"Huh," Brandy continued. "I think you're right. Which makes him resilient, amazing, and sexy—because, you know, he's definitely well put-together."

Steph closed her eyes and sighed. Brandy was right. But so was *she*. And she needed to call Cal back. He'd been nothing but great, and now she'd ghosted him. Well, not fully ghosted him. He'd been out of reach for several days. But apparently, he was back, because he'd left a message on her phone the day before. A message she'd listened to several times if only to appreciate the low rumble of his voice. He'd also texted this morning: *Is everything okay?*

"So . . ." Brandy prompted after the long moment of silence. "Are you bringing him tomorrow to the barbecue?"

"I can't," Steph said. "It will lead him on more. And if I see him in person, it will be too hard to tell him that I'm not interested in his brand of perfect."

Brandy didn't laugh like Steph expected her to. "What's really going on, Steph? You're the one who's usually jilted, and you've been hurt many times because of it. Do you really want to be the one to do that to Cal with no rhyme or reason?"

"I have a lot of reasons." Steph broke down an empty box and tossed it into the garbage pile she was collecting to take to the trash. How she was going to let Cal know he was uninvited to the barbecue, she hadn't decided. She needed to do it today at some point, or he'd just show up at her place tomorrow. She had a hunch he wasn't going to let her ghost him for too much longer.

"Being too amazing isn't a valid reason."

"There are *no* red flags about him," Steph said. "That's a red flag right there."

"Okay, Steph," Brandy said with a sigh. "I can't make you like the guy no matter how great he is."

Steph didn't answer because she *did* like Cal. Maybe even more than like. That's why she wasn't able to see his flaws clearly. With any other guy she'd ever dated, it had been relatively simple to spot their flaws—she'd then decide that they were okay to live with, until the big doozies came along.

"Say hi to my mom for me," Brandy continued in a too-cheerful tone. "Ask if she's dating anyone. She's been denying it, but I still wonder."

"Will do." Steph was grateful for the change of subject.

"Steph?" Carol opened the door to the storage room. "Can you take a haircut walk-in?"

She covered the receiver. "I'm in the middle of stock."

"It can wait." Carol moved away without any further discussion.

"Boss has issued instructions," Steph said into the phone. "I'll report on what your mom says."

She hung up with Brandy, then headed out of the stock room. A man had been led to her salon chair, his profile to her. Dark hair, broad shoulders, bristle on his jaw . . .

Cal.

Well, there was nowhere to hide now. She couldn't go back into the storage room because his gaze had already spotted hers in the mirror. Even though her stomach was doing crazy flips, she walked calmly—sort of—toward him.

"How are you?" she asked. "Helping Rachel today?"

He was studying her and didn't answer. Maybe he'd come to chew her out?

She picked up the black cape she used for all of her clients. "Are you here for a haircut or a shave?" It might sound like a dumb question, but some men came in for a shave if the barber was out for lunch.

"Haircut."

"Okay, then." She draped the covering around him, then snapped it closed at the back of his neck. "Shorter in the same style? Or something new?"

"You choose."

It wasn't the first time she'd received that request, and usually it was from men. But this was Cal. He looked fine—perfect, in fact. And he was still watching her.

She picked up the spray water bottle because she wasn't about to offer him a shampoo, and spritzed water onto his hair.

Still no conversation.

She drew in a breath. "Look, I got your message, Cal," she said as quietly as possible. "Sorry I haven't replied. Things have been crazy."

"No problem."

His voice was more stiff than genuine. She knew it had been a problem. She set down the spray bottle and reached for her comb. "How did your assignment go?"

"Excellent."

Okay . . . so one-word answers were on the menu today. She hoped Lydia would be on time for her appointment, even early, so then Cal would be ushered out the door after paying. Wait. She wouldn't charge him. That would alleviate some of the guilt currently pounding through her chest. "Good, I'm glad."

"Are you?"

Wow . . . Steph almost wanted to call Brandy back and tell her that Cal Conner did have a flaw. A major flaw. He was cold and heartless when he was mad. Of course, the reason why he was mad was because she'd been ignoring him. So it wasn't like she could blame him, and it was a little flattering to think that he was upset over it. Because then it meant he liked her, right? That he cared? But she already knew he did, which wasn't the issue anyway.

She decided not to answer. Instead, she focused on the haircut, even though her fingers felt like blocks of clay. Hopefully he didn't notice her clumsiness. It was perhaps the longest fifteen minutes of her life. When she finished, Lydia was still nowhere in sight.

Steph removed the cape. "It's on the house. You've done plenty of favors for me, so I thought—"

She stopped talking when Cal pulled out a couple of twenties from his wallet and deposited them on the shelf with the hair dryer.

Before she could protest, he stepped close. "When you're ready to give me an explanation of whatever is going on, call me. You have my number." There was no malice in his tone, no anger, just simple words. His dark eyes searched hers for a moment.

"Steph, sorry I'm late," Lydia Kane said, joining the two of them. "Oh, hello." She eyed Cal.

"I'm Cal Conner," he said, sticking out his hand. At least he was being civil to Lydia.

Her eyes rounded. "Oh, so nice to meet you—officially. Thanks again for all your help on my, uh, situation."

"Anytime, Mrs. Kane."

Did he really mean that? Steph wondered.

Before Lydia could strike up more of a conversation, Cal strode out of the salon.

"I guess he was in a hurry?" Lydia said sweetly as she settled into the salon chair.

"Something like that." Steph grabbed the small broom and swept up the bits of Cal's hair. There wasn't much to sweep since she hadn't wanted to change his hairstyle too much.

When she finished and draped Lydia, she was watching Steph through the mirror.

"Rough day?"

Steph blinked and tried to smile, but it didn't quite work. "I think I messed up."

"Oh, honey, we all mess up," Lydia crooned. "If we didn't mess up, then life would be very boring. I can wait here if you need to go say something to that man."

"No, it's all right." Steph was already having a hard time

catching a full breath. She could only imagine what a spectacle it would be chasing down Cal. "He's not in the best of moods."

"I'm sure things will work out just fine—you're both great people," Lydia said. "He was very helpful about that . . . man I dated. Men like Cal are keepers, my dear. My husband was one of those."

"Yes, he was," Steph said, even though she hadn't known Mr. Kane well—mostly she'd heard stories from Brandy. "Did he have personality traits that annoyed you?"

Lydia tilted her head. "Nothing that was a deal breaker, but he always drank out of the top of the milk jug, no matter how many times I told him to get a cup."

"Even when he was sick with a cold or something?"

Lydia arched a brow. "Yes. I grew tired of nagging him, so I bought my own milk and put it on a lower shelf."

"Huh. But that's the only thing that bugged you?"

"That's the only thing I remember." Lydia sighed. "Maybe there were other things, but none of them really mattered. No man will be perfect—but he'll be perfect for you."

Now, Steph felt even more guilty. She was literally holding kindness and generosity against Cal. Because he was too good to be true, that's why. But what if he *was* a good guy through and through? Like Mr. Kane? She thought of Everly's fiancé, Brandy's boyfriend, Julie's husband . . . Steph would never marry any of them, but she couldn't define any major flaws. They were human, men, but perfect for their other halves.

She tried to refocus on her client at hand. "How much do you want cut?"

Lydia skimmed the ends of her hair. "I don't want any of it cut. Only the color touched up at the roots."

"Oh, of course," Steph said. It hadn't been long enough between appointments to do another haircut. She mixed up the color for Lydia, then asked nonchalantly, "How's your dating life?"

"Oh, no you don't," she said, but her tone was teasing. "I know who you're going to rat me out to."

"It was only because I thought there was something off about him—"

"Oh, I know," Lydia cut in. "I'm giving you a hard time. You can tell my daughters that I'm only going to senior socials with friends. No more dating apps or meeting up with practical strangers. If there's something to tell, my daughters will be the first to know."

Steph smiled. "Great. I think that's an excellent plan."

Lydia laughed. They chatted during the color processing, then on Lydia's way out of the salon, she placed a hand on Steph's arm. "Don't worry, dear. Just apologize to that man. He's definitely interested, or he wouldn't have ever come in."

Steph stared after Lydia as she headed out of the salon.

She felt dumb all the way around, or at least that was what she told herself. She somehow made it through the next few clients and kept up a cheerful conversation, all the while thinking that things with Cal were probably beyond repair. But she did owe him an explanation at the very least. No matter how lame it might be.

You're scared. The words pulsed through her.

"I'm not scared," she murmured to herself as she drove home. She wanted a relationship with a great man . . . She was completely normal, and a great catch, if she said so herself. She was sweet, took care of her elderly grandpa, was a fabulous and thoughtful friend, had a good childhood—even though her parents had hightailed it as soon as she graduated—and she spent all day on her feet taking care of others. She constantly put herself out there—socialized, went on dates, tried to give people the benefit of the doubt...

She wasn't purposely trying to push anyone away. She was open to a serious relationship. To having a true boyfriend. And like Lydia had pointed out, there were flaws each person had that could be worked around. And there were good guys all around her... just none that she'd dated, until Cal.

Bottom line, she wasn't scared of Cal, or having a relationship with him. He was just too... much.

You're scared.

The words came again. "I'm scared of what?" she asked the steering wheel. It didn't reply. "Great, now I'm talking to myself."

When she reached home, she found Pops vacuuming the living room floor.

She stopped and stared because she couldn't remember the last time she'd witnessed this. When Pops saw her, he shut off the vacuum. "What? You've never seen a grown man vacuum before?"

"I've seen my dad... but never you."

Pops flashed a grin.

"Good day?" Steph prodded. "No aching knees or stiff shoulders?"

Pops gave a test rotation of his shoulders. "Feeling great, and I have Cal to thank for it."

"Cal?" She couldn't be more surprised, but maybe she wasn't surprised at all. "What does Cal have to do with your aches and pains?"

"He showed me a few stretches that day we painted the fence," Pops said. "And I've been doing them morning and night. They're making a difference."

"Oh wow, I didn't know."

Pops tugged the cord from the outlet and began to wrap it around the vacuum. "There's a lot of things you don't know."

Steph wouldn't say there were a lot of things . . . She lived with Pops, and he wasn't shy about speaking what was on his mind. "Well, I'm glad stretching is helping you. I'm also glad the carpet is clean."

Pops chuckled, then said, "He was worried about you, you know."

Steph paused before entering the kitchen. "Who was worried?"

"Your boyfriend. Stopped by here earlier. Asked if I needed help. Asked how you were doing. What you've been up to." Pops set his hands on his hips. "Did the two of you have an argument or something?"

"No," Steph said automatically, then backtracked. "Cal's not my boyfriend."

Pops let out a low whistle. "Oh boy. I didn't think I'd need to talk to you about this sort of thing. Didn't your parents do the honors?"

"What sort of thing?"

Pops heaved a sigh and rolled the vacuum to the utility closet. Steph watched his movements as her mind turned over the fact that Cal had come to her house. To ask about her. Had he really been *worried*? Just another item to add to his hero list.

Pops moved into the kitchen and sat at the table, so Steph joined him.

"This might be hard for a youngster like you to hear," he began in a firm voice. "And I know I might be old fashioned, but when you spend time with a man, he's going to think you're in a romantic relationship."

Steph sighed. "We're friends, Pops. Men and women can be friends in this century, you know. Not everything has to be about romantic relationships."

Pops's jaw remained in a stubborn line. "It's impossible for a man and woman who like each other romantically to just be friends."

"I don't . . ." She cut herself off. Pops could see right through her. "I do like Cal, but he's . . ."

"He's what?" Pops prompted, his brow furrowing.

Steph couldn't really put it into words and tell him that Cal was too amazing. Pops would laugh her out of the kitchen.

"Love can't be forced," he said in a gravelly tone. "Love happens despite what we might be scared about."

She sucked in a breath. "What would I be scared about?"

Pops shrugged. "Change?"

"Change." Steph laughed. "I'm okay with change. I live with you now, don't I? Every day at the salon is a different day. I go on plenty of dates and have been open to a relationship."

"But not with Cal?" Pops prompted again.

Steph looked down at the table and traced the wood grain. "I just think you like his help around the house."

"That's a lie."

She snapped her head up.

Pops's frown was in place. "I'm not going to turn down good help, but I see the way you watched him. And I see the way he looks at you and responds to you. He's a good man, Steph."

"I know," she said faintly.

"All I'm saying is that he's been bitten before—by family. Lost his mom, eventually lost his dad. And now you're pushing him away. If you're going to cut yourself off from him, then do it completely. It's only fair to both of you. Then take a good look at where you want to be in five years. Ten. Still babysitting me and dating losers? Don't you want more out of your life?"

Steph's eyes filled with hot tears. Was this how her grandpa saw her? Treading water? Accomplishing nothing? And only if she were in a relationship with Cal, or some other man Pops approved of, would she be worth something?

"Look, Pops, sorry to disappoint you so much," she said as calmly as possible. "But I get to decide what to do with my heart. Now, I'm making dinner, and you can do dishes after."

Steph rose and swiped at the now-falling tears. It wasn't her job to be in a relationship with Cal out of pity for his losses. Maybe that wasn't exactly what her grandpa meant, but she did read one thing clear in his speech. She'd led Cal on, and then she ghosted him, and now Pops was interfering . . .

Sixteen

CAL HEARD HIS CELL PHONE ringing, but he was in a message exchange with the law firm that had hired him. Once that was completed, he left his home office and grabbed his phone from where he'd left it on the kitchen table.

Steph had called.

His heart thrummed immediately despite his determination not to react. She was only calling because he'd told her he deserved an explanation. He also wouldn't be surprised if her grandpa had guilted her into it as well.

When he'd gone into the salon earlier today, he wasn't sure what to expect. Or what he'd hoped to gain. It might not have been the right thing to do, but the fact that Steph didn't gush out an apology, or act like her usual affectionate self, told him plenty.

He was okay with being dumped for a date, at least in general, but he didn't like that Steph had gone completely quiet on him. If she didn't feel comfortable telling him no, or telling him she'd changed her mind, it meant she wasn't secure around him.

And that's what bothered him the most.

Steph had been the sunshine in his dark teenaged life.

And seeing her again had brought back all those emotions. Even though they'd lost contact for so long, he'd never forgotten her kindness, her nonjudgment, her sweetness...

But Steph as an adult was carrying burdens she'd only alluded to. Relationship baggage that she hadn't unpacked. When she'd told him about some of the men she'd dated, he could tell she'd taken all their flaws and bullheadedness personally.

There was nothing wrong with Steph. There was everything right about her. So that's why her ghosting bothered him so much. From all of her descriptions of previous dates, she'd been the one who was dumped. So what made him so special now?

Cal settled on the couch, forcing himself to sit in a relaxed position, even though he wanted to pace. Then he called Steph back.

She answered on the third ring. "Hey."

"Hey."

"Thanks for calling me back. Um, I'm sorry about all the miscommunication," she said slowly. "It's been a crazy week, and..."

He waited for her to finish since he wasn't going to jump in and smooth things over like he wanted to.

"Pops told me you stopped by."

"Yes."

"Sorry about that, too—I didn't mean to make you worry."

"I was probably more pissed than worried, Steph," Cal said, unable to hold back any longer. "If you want to tell me no or you've changed your mind, then just say that. You don't need to be all sweet and flirty and kiss me, then ghost me. Just tell me you're done."

Steph didn't say anything for a long moment.

Cal reviewed his words, but decided they'd been exactly what he wanted to say. "Look, I like you. And it's been amazing to see you again. I liked you as a teen, and well, I like you as a grown woman. If you don't feel the same way, then that's fine. Just tell me."

Steph sniffled. Was she crying?

"I do feel the same way, Cal," she said in a trembling voice. "That's the problem."

What was she talking about? "*What's* the problem?"

"I don't want to get my hopes up . . ."

When she didn't finish, he said, "Because you think I'll dump you?"

"I know you'll dump me," Steph said. "It's my track record. And you're . . . well, you're too great of a man to be dumped by. You told me all those men I dated in the past are idiots. That the breakups had nothing to do with me. So if you dump me, then I'll know I can't blame the men I dated for being jerks. I'll know it's all me. Because you're not a jerk or an idiot."

Her logic was twisted, but he could see how she got there. "Well, thanks for telling me I'm not a jerk or idiot, but I can't read the future, Bee," he said in a softer tone. "I'm just willing to take a chance."

Another long moment passed, but he waited it out.

"Why?" she whispered.

Did he not just explain? "I already said I like you—and I might not have all the answers right now, but I'm okay with that. I'd rather have questions and still spend time with you."

"See? Even when I've been a jerk to you, you're still being sweet to me."

Cal closed his eyes. He wished he were in the same room with her. This conversation wasn't ideal over the phone. "You say it like it's a bad thing."

"Every relationship has taught me that the other shoe will drop," Steph said. "So I guess it's easier if I drop it myself, because if I allow myself to put hope in a relationship with you, I know there will be pain in the end."

Ah, he understood exactly what she meant. "I'm scared, too."

"You are?" She sounded surprised.

"Of course." Cal rose from the couch and crossed to the windows. "I mean, I didn't expect to have feelings return when I saw you at the reunion. I wanted to apologize, sure, but I didn't expect... *you.*"

"This is crazy, Cal," she whispered.

"I agree." He breathed a little easier, but his pulse was still racing. "It's crazy, but I want to find out where this goes. Where *we* might go." He might as well put it all out there—so she could take it or leave it. If she left it, he'd find a way to move on.

Steph was quiet for so long, Cal thought she might have hung up. When she finally spoke, he was more than glad she hadn't. "Cal, I'm kind of a mess. I don't even know how to have a relationship."

"I don't think you're a mess, Bee. And I don't know if I know how to have a relationship either," he said. "Technically, I've spent more time with your grandpa than you."

Steph laughed, and it was the most beautiful sound he'd heard all week. It also gave him hope again.

"True, you need to do something about that."

He chuckled. "Just tell me what to do, and I'll do it. I know that theories say men and women can't truly be friends, but maybe we could test it out." Was that desperate sounding? He didn't care if it was.

Her sigh was soft over the phone. "How are you so great?"

"You mean considering where I come from?"

"No, that's not what I meant at all," Steph quickly said. "It's just that . . . none of my past male friends or dates would care so much about Pops. It's very endearing."

"I like him," Cal said. "It's that simple. Well, not exactly that simple because I'm pretty sure you're the major driving force behind it all."

He heard the smile in her voice when she replied, "You need to tone it down. Your charm is going to my head."

"Hmm. I'll keep that in mind." He paused. "So, what do you think about the friendship thing?"

"You want me to friend zone you?"

"No, but if that's what it takes to keep hanging out together, I'm good with that."

"That's very magnanimous of you," Steph said, amusement in her tone. "You're going to have to prove it. And no flirting."

That might be easier said than done, but Cal was all in. "Fine. What are you doing tonight?"

"Chilling in bed and reading," she said. "Hoping that Pops will do the same and watch a game on TV or something since he's been bragging about the stretching exercises you taught him and doing chores like a madman."

Cal laughed. "Oh really?"

"He was vacuuming when I came home from work."

"Oh wow. Earning his keep. But his activities aren't what I'm interested in. Want to go get ice cream somewhere? As friends, of course."

"You know Everly Falls is a small town," she said. "By the time you get here, everything will be closed."

"Hmm. I could bring some ice cream from my freezer."

He sensed her hesitation, but at least it hadn't been an automatic no.

"But you already drove here once today."

That he did. "You could check out Grandin, then."

She didn't speak for a moment, and he didn't give her a counteroffer.

"Okay."

His pulse leapt. "Wait, really?"

She laughed. "I can leave Everly Falls once in a while . . . for a friend."

He grinned and turned to scan his place. Everything was pretty clean. "You're not too tired to drive?"

"I'm fine," she said. "I'll get ready and head over. It's time I put a little skin in the game."

"I like where this is going."

"Whatever." He heard the smile in his voice. "Text me your address."

Cal did, and he would be lying if he said he wasn't counting the minutes, since he knew exactly how long the drive was. Would she stick to the speed limit? What time had she actually left? Would she encounter any traffic? Likely not.

He also happened to be watching out the window when she pulled her car into the parking lot. He continued watching when she climbed out, looked up to check out the numbers on the town houses, then headed toward his. She wore a navy dress, long boots, and a light-brown scarf. Her hair was pulled back into a ponytail.

"Breathe normally," he whispered to himself. It was a pretty big deal for Steph to be coming over to his place—he supposed it was part of their relationship progressing, or at least he hoped that's what it meant. Somehow their conversation had changed Steph's mind about them, and he was determined not to take any backward steps tonight.

Let her take the lead. In everything. Keep the ball in her court. For real.

When Cal opened the door to her knock, he again told himself to be casual, normal. But then she stepped close and hugged him. His breath left his lungs, and relief shuddered through him. He'd missed her more than he'd allowed himself to feel.

"Hi," he whispered.

"Hi." She drew away enough to look up at him and smile. "Were you watching out the window?"

"Uh, yes?"

"I thought I saw movement." She stepped back and unwound the scarf about her neck. "You're funny. Now show me your place."

"Okay . . ." Just like that, he was giving her a tour.

"So this is where all the magic happens," Steph said, walking into his home office. "Nice computer stuff."

Cal had a couple of processors and monitors set up. He watched her walk about the room. It was strange to have her in his space, but he liked it.

"What's the hardest case you've ever investigated?" Steph turned to face him from where she stood by the windows. The sun had already set, leaving a pale orange sky behind her, and making her hair a deeper red.

"I don't think I could pinpoint just one," Cal said. "Anything that involves kids is always rough. They get caught in the middle of divorces and are used as pawns. Nothing about that is fair."

"I don't doubt it." She exhaled and moved to his desk. "You have a lot of security badges."

He did. A pile of them sat in a small box on his desk. "Makes me look official, trustworthy, I guess. No one really reads the fine print."

She picked up one and turned it over. "What's the most dangerous situation you've been in?" Her eyes lifted to his.

He liked that she was truly interested, but he could only talk about his clients in general. "I haven't been hired to rat out violent criminals, if that's what you're asking. I don't consider myself in physical danger, just maybe in danger of being noticed, and the work getting delayed or having to quit the case because the actions of the person will change if they know they're being tracked. Or they'll flee the state or country."

"Huh." Steph set down the badge and folded her arms. "So you could find out anything about me without me knowing it?"

Where was this going? "I could—but I don't think I have reason to. You've been an open book, plus I doubt you have any dark secrets."

She straightened. "You're right. I'm pretty boring." She threw him a smirk, then headed past him and walked into the kitchen. "What kind of ice cream do you have?"

Cal laughed and turned to follow her. "Interrogation is over? You don't want to ask me about my dark secrets?"

She had opened the freezer door. "Do you have any?" She pulled out a carton of ice cream and turned to face him, her ponytail swinging.

"None that I can think of—you know the most about me out of everyone." He walked around the island and grabbed a couple of bowls from the cupboard, then two spoons from a drawer.

He took the ice cream carton from her and began to dish it up.

Steph leaned against the counter near him and watched him work. "What are your flaws?"

He met her blue gaze. "Isn't that relative?"

She lifted a shoulder. "Maybe. But I want to know why you're not in a relationship or married. You acted surprised that I wasn't."

Just Add Friendship

Cal slid a bowl of ice cream toward Steph, then picked up his own. After taking a bite, he said, "So you want to know what complaints other women have had about me?"

Steph flashed a smile. "Exactly." She took a bite of her ice cream. "This is really good. I'm glad you invited me over."

He turned to lean against the counter next to her. "I'm glad you came."

Steph smirked. "Tell me why you're single, Cal. Do you dump women left and right?"

He set his bowl down. "No . . . things just didn't feel right with other women I've dated, you know?"

She met his gaze, then looked away. "I don't really know, because I don't really trust my feelings."

"Maybe since I'm more closed off than you, when I do feel something, it's more obvious. You're the only person I've told the full story of my life to. With other women I dated, I didn't ever go into any detail."

Her gaze slid back to his, and her smile appeared.

The smile that he loved and that told him he hadn't scared her off by his confession.

"You've told me a lot of details." She set down her bowl of ice cream.

"That's correct."

She tipped her head. "Because you feel things for me? Or because we're friends?"

He couldn't help but return her smile, even though nerves were bouncing around like crazy. "I'm pleading the Fifth."

Seventeen

EATING ICE CREAM AND FLIRTING with Cal in his kitchen was definitely one of Steph's favorite activities. Who knew?

She'd spent most of the drive over to his place on her Bluetooth talking to Brandy about this man. Brandy definitely endorsed him, and she said one thing that Steph found significant. If she didn't open her heart, then she'd never know if Cal was the real deal.

She had a feeling he was the real deal. No matter how much she'd pushed that thought away over the past week. But she was going to stick to her conviction of keeping Cal in the friend zone. She wasn't about to jump over relationship hurdles that would lead to her tripping and falling.

"When you see Cal's place, you'll know more about him and if there are things you can't live with," Brandy had told her. "I can't explain it, but you'll know."

"Like laundry climbing up the walls?"

"You might not know that unless you go into his bedroom," Brandy said with a laugh.

Steph scoffed. "I'm not planning on that thorough of a tour." Still, when she'd walked around his town house, she only saw an orderly and somewhat stark environment. It fit him, and nothing bothered her. Except that he only had one kind of ice cream in his freezer. Who did that? A person needed at least three flavors to cater to moods.

"Friends can't plead the Fifth," Steph said to Cal as they stood next to each other, leaning against his counter.

She liked him in the evening-at-home look, with his bare feet, faded jeans, old T-shirt, and rumpled hair. Some men grew more handsome with age, and Cal was definitely that man. She had to stop herself from lifting her hand and touching his new haircut. Had it only been this afternoon that he'd been at the salon?

"I don't want to scare you off," Cal said, his gaze steady on hers. "I just barely got out of being ghosted, and now we're officially friends."

"True." Steph moved a couple of inches closer until their arms were nearly touching. "I'm glad you didn't ghost me back."

His dark eyes searched hers. "Are you?"

"I'm here, aren't I?"

His smile was slow. "That you are."

Her heart flipped, and she knew that if she didn't put some space between her and this man, she'd break the friend zone by kissing him. She shifted away from him and took another bite of her cold ice cream, hoping it would cool everything else off. She might need another scoop. The next bite gave her brain freeze, and she winced.

"Are you okay?" Cal asked.

Steph waved her spoon. "Ate too fast."

He smiled. "In a hurry?"

"No . . ." The deep ache eased, and she said, "It was getting too warm in here."

"Yeah, for me, too," he said easily, although the intensity in his eyes made other things clear. "More ice cream?"

"Maybe something else."

His brows rose. "What do you have in mind?"

"Maybe you can show me around Grandin." She set her bowl in the kitchen sink and turned on the faucet to rinse it out. Busyness and distraction were great. "I want to see the places where you used to live—you know, the diner."

Cal joined her at the sink, and his nearness once again set her pulse jumping. "Okay."

Once the bowls were rinsed out, they left the town house and headed toward the parking lot. A car pulled up, and a woman climbed out.

"Hi, Cal," she said in a friendly tone. She smoothed back her curly dark hair that was trying to escape a headband.

"Got the kids with you?"

"Yep, and they're cranky."

Cal chuckled. "Bedtime, right?"

"Right." The woman set a hand on her hip. "Who's this?"

"This is Steph—from my high school days. Steph, this is Diane."

The women nodded and smiled at each other.

"Hi, Cal!" a small voice called from inside the car.

Cal stopped and opened the door as the mother helped out a little girl from the other side.

The little boy on Cal's side was a dark-haired kid, about four years old.

"Hey, Jeff," he said. They knuckle bumped. "What's up?"

Jeff's forehead creased. "My sister can't sing my favorite song."

"Oh, that's great news," Cal said with a smile. "That means you can be the one to teach her the right way to sing it."

The kid's expression cleared. "Yeah!"

Just Add Friendship

Steph watched their easy exchange with amusement. In a few minutes, Diane had her kids out of the car. The young girl hugged Cal fiercely around the legs. He patted her head, and she beamed up at him. The siblings were obviously twins.

It was all very cute.

Steph signed inwardly. Cal was very cute.

When he said goodbye to his neighbors, he turned back to Steph.

"Cute family," she said. "Good neighbors?"

"Great neighbors," Cal said with a smile. "I babysit sometimes, and Diane pays me back with food."

"Ah, you're not hard to please."

"I'm picky in some things." He unlocked his nearby car and opened the door for her.

"We're not walking?"

"It's a couple of miles," Cal said. "These town houses are at the edge of the new development that surrounds the town."

She slipped into the car, noting again how he kept things clean and organized. When he settled in the car next to her, Steph asked, "How long have you been neighbors with Diane's family?"

Cal put the car into reverse. "Maybe a year? There are new transplants coming to Grandin, and they're one of them."

Steph settled into the coziness of the car, and they drove in silence until they neared town, and Cal began to narrate the different locations.

They slowed on Main Street and parked in front of the post office. "Come on, we'll walk the rest of the way to the diner."

"Is it still open this time of night?"

"Yeah," he said.

Steph walked alongside him, wondering what it might have felt like to be teenaged Cal on the run. Not having a plan or knowing where he'd sleep or eat next. Soon the diner came into view. The large windows in front showed that it was nearly empty.

"The high school kids come to the place after sport games," Cal said, "so that might be pretty soon." He opened the door for Steph and ushered her in.

The first thing she noticed was the smell of hot food. The diner was spotless, with gleaming floors and scrubbed tables and booths. Framed black-and-white pictures of an older Grandin lined the walls above the booths.

A short, balding man came out of the kitchen and spotted Cal. "My man, you're here." The man's hazel eyes zeroed in on Steph. "Who's your lady?"

"Bruce, this is Steph," Cal said. "We go way back to high school."

Bruce's bushy brows lifted. "You mean before you came here?"

"Yep."

He wiped his hands on his black apron and shook Steph's hand. "Great to meet you."

She grasped his thick, sturdy hand. "You as well."

Bruce nodded toward the row of booths. "Have a seat anywhere. The meal is on the house."

"Oh, we're not here to eat," Cal said, then looked at Steph. "Unless you're hungry?"

"No, I'm good."

Cal nodded, then shifted his attention back to Bruce. "I'm showing Steph around the town, so we're just stopping in."

Bruce flashed a smile. "Want to see the back storage room where you used to sleep?"

"No," he said at the same time Steph said, "Sure."

Cal groaned. "It's nothing like it was."

Bruce smirked, motioning them to follow him. "It's at least interesting... This way."

Steph and Cal followed him past the kitchen area. Bruce stopped before a plain brown door and opened it, then tugged at an overhead string to turn on the dangling light bulb.

The small room, lined with metal shelves, contained bins and boxes of foodstuff. Even if everything was cleared out, there wouldn't be much room for a mattress, especially for a tall teenager.

"This is it, huh?" Steph said, feeling huge in the small space.

"The harbor where I finally got my head in the right place."

"That's right, and we were happy to have you." Bruce stepped back. "I'll be in the kitchen if you change your minds about eating."

"Thanks, man," Cal said.

With Bruce gone, he turned to Steph and eyed her. "What do you think?"

What did she think about Cal sleeping in a room not much bigger than a closet? She wanted to grieve for what he'd gone through as a kid, but the man standing in front of her was a product of all of that—and she could see the resiliency in his eyes.

"I think you're amazing."

One of his brows arched. "I was lucky."

"Like I said, amazing." She moved forward and hugged him. How could she not? When his arms came around her to hug her back, she told herself that friends could hug anytime and that didn't mean her heart had to race, or her pulse thrum.

She drew back. The room was really very small and getting warmer. "Is it weird to be here?"

"Kind of." He gave a small shrug. "It always took me a while to fall asleep. Sometimes thinking about hanging out with you or wondering what you were doing were my safer thoughts."

Steph's throat tightened. "Really?"

"As a friend, of course—all of my thoughts were platonic."

Steph laughed at that. "Sure they were."

He was smiling, and she was probably blushing, but she was mostly happy he could tease when referring to his teenaged trauma.

Voices reached them, coming from the front of the restaurant. "There's the high school crowd," Cal said, moving to the door. "We'd better get out of their way."

They thanked Bruce and headed outside again. As they walked along the sidewalk, Cal continued pointing places out and telling her stories of his experiences. As he talked, she realized he hadn't had any sort of normal high school experience. First, his mother had died, then his father had neglected and abused him, then he ended up in Everly Falls without any parents and mostly on his own, then he'd been completely homeless. At the mercy of a stranger's kindness.

As they headed back to the car, she said, "I don't know how many times I can tell you that you're amazing, Cal."

"Can there be too many times?" he teased, throwing her a grin.

"You've pushed through life no matter what's thrown at you," Steph said in a more sober tone. "You jump in and help people—no questions asked. And no whining."

"I definitely whine—at least in my head."

Steph laughed. "Oh really? What kind of things do you whine about?"

Just Add Friendship

"Mostly about food—you know if I overcook or undercook, or the order is delayed when I call for delivery."

"Ah, that's a true flaw, then," Steph said. They'd reached the car, and Cal opened the passenger-side door for her. She had the urge to hug him again, but instead, she climbed into the car.

She'd left her cell on the seat, and there were a couple of missed-call alerts. Both from Pops. She called him as Cal started the engine, but no one answered.

"Everything okay?" Cal asked.

"Pops called, but he's not answering," she said, worry climbing her throat. "He didn't leave a message either." She called his number again, letting it ring until it went into his creaky voice mail.

"Is there someone who can check on him?"

"Yeah." Steph's mind was already going there, and she called Lori since Brandy lived above Everly Falls, a good twenty minutes from the house. "Hey, sorry to bother you, but I'm in Grandin. Pops called me a couple of times when I didn't have my phone. And now he's not answering."

"I can head over right now," Lori said, concern in her voice. "Why are you in Grandin? Oh wait . . . Are you with Cal?" Her voice had turned sugary, although Steph could also hear the sounds of Lori getting into a car and starting it up.

"Yes, but we can talk about that later," Steph said. "Let me know what's going on as soon as you see Pops."

"Will do." Lori hung up, and Steph closed her eyes, silently praying.

Please be okay. Please.

Cal grasped her hand. "I can take you back right now."

Steph released a breath. "I'll drive myself. I don't want to worry about shuffling cars later. I just need Lori to call me and say that Pops fell asleep in front of the TV."

"Right." He squeezed her hand and released it. "That's probably exactly what happened."

By the time they made it back to Cal's town house, Lori still hadn't called. Steph couldn't wait anymore, so she called her. No answer.

"I'm going to start driving," she said. "Every minute will bring me closer to home."

"Steph, let me drive you. It's not a big deal to take a bus or something back here tomorrow," he said. "I don't want you driving while dealing with so much."

Steph bit her lip. The offer was so generous. She wanted to say no. She wanted to jump in her car and drive as fast as she dared, but maybe Cal was right.

"Okay, but can we go right now?"

"Of course," he said, and they detoured toward her car.

Steph didn't even ask him if he needed to get anything from his place. They jumped in her car, with Cal in the driver's seat.

It was another ten minutes before Lori finally called. "Steph?" she said, her voice high, panicked. "Pops had a fall. He's talking and everything, but he was really shaken up. I called the ambulance, and they're taking him to the hospital."

Steph couldn't speak for a moment. "Did he tell you what happened?"

"He was pretty fuzzy on the details," Lori said. "I had to go through the back door, and I found him in the kitchen. The phone was too far for him to reach. I guess he fell and was able to get to the phone, then fell again and dropped it."

Steph reached for Cal's hand and held on tight. "Why did he fall? Did he break a bone?"

"It was all kind of a blur. I'm sorry. I don't think the paramedics knew exactly what had happened either."

"Okay," she said, her thoughts spinning all over. "Cal's driving me back home, and we'll go straight to the hospital."

"I'll meet you there."

Steph's instinct was to tell her no, not to worry about it, but instead, she said, "That would be great. Thank you so much."

When she hung up, she looked over at Cal and told him what Lori had said. "Do you think it was a stroke?"

"Maybe," he said. "The fact that he's talking is great, though, and I'm glad Lori found him when she did."

Steph nodded as everything began to sink in. "I'm glad he was able to call and alert me."

"I'm sorry," Cal said softly.

Guilt washed over her. Guilt and pain that something might be seriously wrong with Pops. If she'd stayed home tonight, he would have been fine. Right? She'd spent those two nights babysitting Maren, and nothing had happened to Pops. Why did she have to be so far away when it did?

"It's not your fault," Cal told her, as if he could read her mind.

"You don't know that," Steph said. It wasn't fair to say, but until she had answers, she did feel like it was her fault. "I need to call my parents."

She hated to wake them up, but what if the worst happened? They'd be more upset if she didn't inform them.

"What did the doctor say?" her mother asked right away.

"I haven't spoken to a doctor yet, but I'll let you know what's going on as soon as I find out at the hospital."

"We can catch a flight tomorrow," her father said.

"Not until we know what's going on," her mother cut in. "I don't want to spend money on last-minute plane tickets unless we have to. I do want to know, Stephenie, why weren't you home this time of night?"

Because she was a grown woman and wasn't in lockdown. "I was visiting a friend in Grandin." She avoided any probing questions, then promised again to let her parents know as soon as she had more details. After hanging up with them, she reached for Cal's hand because it was the only thing keeping her from completely melting.

Eighteen

THE HOSPITAL IN EVERLY FALLS was quickly becoming familiar to Cal since he'd been here multiple times in the last couple of weeks. Once he parked Steph's car, he hurried into the building with her.

"You're here," Lori said, rising from the lobby chairs. She stepped forward and hugged Steph. "I told the others, and they'll be here in a heartbeat if you need them."

"Thanks for coming," Steph said. "I need to find out what's going on first."

"No problem." Lori looked like she might have been crying, or just spooked, but she walked with them to the reception area.

The woman at the front desk told them which room Pops was in. "Only two visitors at a time."

"I'll wait here," Lori said quickly.

Cal and Steph headed down the corridor.

"It's a good sign that he's in a room, right?" she asked, her voice quaking with what must be exhaustion and worry. "Not having an emergency operation?"

Cal glanced over at her. In the past hour, she'd voiced all of her concerns about Pops, as if speaking everything aloud helped her process the information.

"Yes, that's how I'm taking it, too," he said. "No one is tougher than your grandpa."

Steph nodded stiffly, then turned a corner. Pops's strident voice could be heard.

Cal almost smiled, except Pops was saying, "I want the sweatpants my granddaughter bought me last Christmas. This scrap of cloth isn't for a grown man. It doesn't even reach my knees."

Steph hurried forward and practically sprinted into the room. "Pops! Are you okay?"

Cal was right behind her. Pops reclined on a hospital bed, flanked by two nurses, his spindly legs sticking out from a blue-checked hospital gown. One of the nurses was trying to cover him with a blanket, but he kept pushing it aside.

"Oh, there you are," he said to Steph. "Can you tell these ladies that I'm fine and need to go home now? I can't sleep in this wobbly bed. Besides, it smells like a bowling alley in here."

Steph ignored his complaints and moved to his bedside. She leaned down and hugged him, then kissed the top of his head. "What happened, Pops?"

Her soft tone seemed to calm his agitation.

"You didn't answer your phone."

"I know, Pops, I'm sorry," Steph said, grasping his hand. "I'm glad you remembered to call me, though. Did you slip and fall?"

"I felt dizzy, I guess," he said. "I got back up and called you, but then it happened again."

As he spoke, Steph covered his legs with the blanket that the nurses had been attempting to give him.

"I stood up too fast. There's no reason for them to keep me in the hospital."

"They want to run some tests to make sure you're okay," Steph said. "See if there's anything they need to know about."

"I'm old, that's all it is." His gaze shifted past her to Cal. "Guess you made up with your boyfriend?"

Cal chuckled because Steph blushed, and Pops was grinning.

"We're still friends, if that's what you're asking, sir," he said, moving to stand next to her. "How are you feeling, buddy?"

"Perfectly fine," Pops quipped, waving a hand that sported a hospital bracelet at the wrist. "A whole lot of fuss, if you ask me."

"Might be," Cal said. "But it's better to figure stuff out now than later."

Pops's eyes shifted toward the ceiling. "I suppose you're right." When he looked back at Cal, he said, "Now, can you talk these nurses into turning on the game?"

"I think I can manage that."

Steph updated her parents, then texted Lori it was okay for her to go home. They stayed in the hospital room with Pops for the next hour, which was interrupted by blood pressure checks. Even Aunt Rachel stopped in after Cal texted her. She was on duty anyway, and she was able to answer some questions for Steph since the doctor wouldn't be back in again until the morning.

"We don't think he had a stroke because he seems to move and speak fine—at least for his age," Rachel told the both of them after Pops finally fell asleep. "We need to figure out if the dizziness was medicine related or something else. Because of his age, we're keeping him overnight."

"That makes sense," Steph said. "Can I stay the night in his room? I know there's only a chair, but I worry that he'll wake up in a panic."

Rachel put a hand on her arm. "He'll be in good hands. We'll be checking on him regularly, and if there's an emergency, the hospital will call you."

Steph released a slow breath. "Okay." She glanced over at Pops, who was sleeping soundly. "I'll come over first thing in the morning."

Rachel squeezed her shoulder. "That sounds fine. Now, you get some sleep. We'll take care of him on our end."

Steph finally relented and left the room with Cal.

He slipped his arm about her shoulders as they walked through the empty hospital lobby. "I think the news is the best it can be," he said.

Steph nodded, but didn't say anything, only leaned into him.

When they reached her car, she paused. "Thanks for everything you're doing, Cal. Driving me. Having Rachel come talk to us—" Her voice broke.

"Hey, come here." He pulled her close, and she let him hug her.

"Sorry," she whispered.

"No apologies allowed. You're tired and wrung out. Let's go to your place and follow my sister's orders. Get some sleep."

She lifted her head.

"I'll take the couch."

Her brows arched, and he smoothed back some stray hair from her face. "Come on, you need sleep."

The streets of Everly Falls were completely silent as they drove to Steph's place.

Cal straightened up a few things in the house while she got ready for bed. Soon, she brought him a blanket and pillow.

"You can use Pops's bed if you want."

"It's fine," Cal said. "Too close to you—and tempting."

She gave him a small smile. "Do I need to lock my door?"

He wanted to pull her close, kiss her, and tell her he was already tired of the friend zone. "No. I'll pretend the floor is hot lava."

She laughed. "Whatever helps you out. See you in the morning."

Cal didn't sleep for a long time after he heard her bedroom door shut. He worried about Pops, sure, but he was worried about Steph, too. She was juggling a lot on her own, and even though his aunt Rachel had been a fierce woman living on her own, too, she wasn't taking care of an elderly person on top of that. Not that Cal the teenager had been easy at all . . .

It felt like he'd just fallen asleep when he heard an alarm go off. The sound was faint, but it was definitely an alarm. Steph must have set it. He moved to a sitting position and parted the drapes on the other side of the couch. Barely dawn.

Stifling a yawn, he rose and folded the blanket, then went to find the bathroom that Steph said he could use.

After a quick shower, he came out into the hallway to find her waiting for him. Showered and dressed and folding her arms.

"Am I late?"

"I didn't think you'd take such a long shower."

In Cal's estimation, he'd been in the bathroom for twenty minutes—but that was because he'd shaved.

"Had to get pretty."

Her expression softened. "Well, it worked. Come on. I want to see how Pops is doing."

"No breakfast?"

She paused and looked back at him. "The hospital has a cafeteria."

"Right." Cal decided that Steph must not be a breakfast

eater or really a morning person at all. He'd have to convince her otherwise, since breakfast could be the best, most enjoyable and relaxing meal of the day.

This time, she drove, and it turned out that he didn't get breakfast in the cafeteria after all. Pops was being examined by the doctor when they arrived at his hospital room.

"You need to write all of that down for my granddaughter, so she doesn't forget my appointments," he said.

"Write what down?" Steph asked.

The doctor and Pops turned to look at them.

"Hi, I'm Dr. Wright." The woman in dark green scrubs held out her hand to shake Steph's.

Steph greeted her and introduced Cal.

"He can stay, if you're asking, Doc," Pops said. "He's practically family."

Dr. Wright nodded, then turned her attention to Steph. "Have you noticed anything off with your grandfather's balance lately or issues with vertigo?"

"I don't use a cane, if that's what you're asking," Pops volunteered.

"He has some better days than others," Steph conceded. "But lately, he's been doing a lot more chores around the house."

The doctor nodded. "We tested for BPPV this morning, which is benign paroxysmal positional vertigo. It looks like your grandfather is a good candidate for physical therapy."

"Oh wow, okay," Steph said. "And that will help his vertigo?"

"Yes," Dr. Wright said. "It should help tremendously."

While Steph continued speaking to the doctor, Pops motioned for Cal to come closer.

He raised his brows, but followed the bidding.

"Tell them I want to go home today," Pops whispered.

"The hospital food is atrocious. Wouldn't feed it to a criminal."

Cal chuckled. "I'll be sure to let them know of your wishes."

"Thank you." Pops patted his arm. "You're a good man. I'm glad that you and Steph made peace."

Cal wondered what all Steph had told her grandpa about him, but that got shoved to the back of his mind when Dr. Wright turned to them and said, "Well, there's no reason you can't be discharged this morning."

"Hallelujah!" Pops punched his fists into the air.

Dr. Wright simply smiled. "A nurse will come in soon with the paperwork. Someone will be calling you later today to set up an appointment schedule for your physical therapy."

It was a full hour before Cal and Steph were walking out of the hospital, with Pops riding in a wheelchair. Cal helped him into the front seat of Steph's car.

"I can't believe they want me to do physical therapy every day," he said. "Who has time for that?"

Cal knew it would be a huge undertaking for Steph, and he planned to talk her into getting some help—from friends or neighbors, or even having one of her parents fly in.

"This place looks different," Pops said as they helped him into the house. "What did you do? Paint or something?"

"Nothing's different, Pops," Steph said. "You just haven't left the house in a while so you're probably seeing things with new eyes."

"The place needs painting," he continued. "See how dingy the walls are? They used to be white."

Steph cut a glance to Cal and gave a slight shake of her head.

"I wasn't even going to offer," he said quietly.

A smile appeared on her face, but it didn't erase the tired lines about her eyes.

"Boy, I'm starving," Pops declared as he moved from the living room to the kitchen. "Do we have any leftovers?"

"I can make something fresh," Steph said.

"Let me cook," Cal offered. "I'm a pro breakfast maker."

"Well, it's about time you carried some weight around here," Pops said.

Steph winced, but Cal laughed. "Prepare yourself for the best French toast you've had in your life."

Pops eased into his recliner, folding his hands atop his belly. "Sounds like an excellent plan." Then he switched on the remote and surfed through channels. "Morning TV is a waste. Hope there's an old game on."

Steph followed Cal into the kitchen and sidled up to him as he opened the refrigerator door. "You have eggs and milk, right?" he asked.

"Yes, but you don't have to cook, Cal," she said. "Don't you need to look up bus schedules?"

He looked over at her. "Trying to get rid of me?"

Her cheeks pinked. "No. I just don't want . . . you've already done so much."

Cal grasped her hand and enfolded her fingers. "Didn't we already have this talk? We're friends, you know, and if Lori or Brandy or Julie were here, would you turn down their cooking?"

Her mouth parted, and her blue eyes filled with tears. "No . . . but you've done so much. I mean, you drove me home, you had to sleep on that awful couch, and—"

"Bee, I'm glad to be here, and I'm glad to help." He squeezed her hand.

She looked down at their intertwined hands, then seemed to relax a little, until his stomach growled.

"Is that you?" she asked with a laugh, stepping away.

"Yep." He smiled and reached for the eggs.

Steph cut up strawberries as he started grilling the French toast.

When he caught her watching him, appreciation in her gaze, he said, "See, breakfast isn't so bad."

She gave a little shake of her head. "I still can't believe you're here. I'm not used to . . ."

When her voice trailed off, he supplied, "Help?"

"Yeah." Her expression turned sheepish.

"Speaking of help," he said. "What are the plans to get Pops back and forth to his appointments?"

"Oh." Steph waved a hand. "I'll talk to the Carol at the salon and rearrange my schedule."

Cal decided to bite his tongue, for now.

Nineteen

Over their meal of French toast, Steph's phone kept buzzing, until she finally had to turn it off. "Sorry," she said.

"What are your friends yapping about now?" Pops asked, then took another huge bite of breakfast. It seemed his appetite was back in full force.

"They're asking about you, Pops," Steph said. "And chatting about the barbecue they'd planned."

She felt Cal's gaze on her.

"You kids going?" Pops asked.

Steph frowned. "No, I already told them I'm not leaving you alone."

He waved a hand. "I'm as good as new."

"Whatever, Pops," she said. "You were in the hospital an hour ago."

"What if we take him?" Cal said. "I can stay another night, and he can get out a little. Then you won't have to cancel on your friends."

"It might be too taxing on Pops—"

"I'd love to go," he cut in, holding up a piece of French toast speared on a fork. "Isn't it at Ian Hudson's cabin? I've wanted to see what he's done with that place."

Steph looked from Pops to Cal. "Are you serious?"

Both men said "yes" at the same time.

"All right," she said, holding back a surprised laugh. "I'll text them."

"If they say no about letting me crash the party, that's okay," Pops said. "I've got a game to catch up on."

"They already said yes." Steph reached for her phone to turn it back on. "They suggested it when I backed out." She texted her friend group. *We're coming after all. Pops, too. I'll put together a dessert.*

"Well, there you go." Pops chuckled as if he were pleased with himself. "It's been a while since I've had some good old-fashioned barbecue." He looked pointedly at Steph. "No offense."

"No offense taken." She eyed her grandpa. "But I think you should take a nap first. The hospital put you through the wringer."

Pops gave an approving nod. "She's a master planner," he said to Cal, who only smiled. "I guess that's my hint to give you some alone time."

"Pops, that's not what I meant." Steph's cheeks had warmed, and she avoided looking at Cal.

But Cal nudged her leg with his knee under the table.

She finally looked over at him, and felt something in her chest hitch. Gratitude flooded through her. If she was going to be teased about anyone, she was happy it was Cal.

Once their meal was over, he said, "I'll clean up, and you can help Pops get situated."

"I can manage." Pops slapped his hands on the table, then pushed himself up from the chair.

He swayed a little, and Steph hurried to his side.

"I stood too fast," he mumbled, but he still accepted her arm as they walked down the hall.

She walked him into his bedroom, where he insisted on

taking everything from there. But still she waited outside the door, until he called out, "My head's on the pillow. You can stop spying on me now. Tell that man of yours thanks for his help today."

"All right, Pops, have a good nap. Love you."

He mumbled something that sounded like, "Love you, too."

Steph headed down the hall, smiling to herself. Once she reached the kitchen, she paused to watch Cal washing the dishes. Just as he said he would.

She wanted to cross the room and wrap her arms about his waist from behind. Instead, she stayed put and said, "Thanks for doing that, Cal."

He looked over his shoulder. "No thanks needed."

"I disagree."

She walked slowly toward him, her heart pounding. "Pops thinks you walk on water."

Cal smirked. "I'm only doing dishes."

Steph leaned against the counter close to him. "Among other things . . ." Then she stifled a yawn.

"You should take a nap," Cal said, rinsing off the suds from his hands. "Maybe I will, too."

"Sorry I don't have more than the couch to offer you."

"It's fine, really." He grabbed a dish towel and dried his hands. "You go and I'll finish up in here."

"You're spoiling me too much," she said, wondering if she was getting way too comfortable with all this friend-zone stuff. "I'm going to get used to it."

"Fine with me." Cal nudged her away. "See you later."

She smirked. "Fine." Steph headed down the hallway again, and before she settled on her bed, she silenced her phone. She didn't know if she'd be able to nap in the middle of the day—it would be a novelty.

But somehow she fell asleep, and when Cal tapped on her bedroom door, it took her a moment to remember all that had gone on.

She pushed up on her elbows. "Is Pops okay?"

"He's fine," Cal said from the doorway, clearly keeping himself out of her bedroom. "We're getting ready for the barbecue, and I didn't know how much time you needed."

"What time is it?"

"Almost five o'clock."

Steph stifled a yawn. "Okay, thanks for waking me. I can't believe I slept." She met his dark eyes, which were taking in the whole of her and her bed. "Did you sleep?"

"No, but I got some work done, so it's fine."

Steph climbed off the bed and smoothed back her hair. "Everything all right?"

"Yeah," Cal said. "I don't have any real commitments until Monday, when I have a conference call with a new client."

"Dagnammit," a voice sailed from somewhere in the house. "This thing isn't working."

"What's he doing?" Steph asked.

"We were making dessert."

"Oh, dessert." She hurried past him into the hallway. "I forgot."

Cal grasped her arm. "It's fine. We're almost done."

Something clattered on the floor in the direction of the kitchen.

"Or not," he said, moving with Steph along the hallway.

They arrived in the kitchen to see Pops standing above a bowl that had splattered dark batter all over the floor.

"Brownies?" Steph guessed.

"Used to be," Pops grumbled. He bent to pick up the bowl, and both Cal and Steph rushed forward.

"I'll get that," she said.

"Here, you sit down," Cal said, taking Pops's arm.

"I'm not some kind of glass flower," he protested.

But Pops sat at the kitchen table anyway while Steph and Cal made short work of cleaning up.

"Let's stop at the store and grab some good old-fashioned root beer and vanilla ice cream," Cal said.

Steph looked over at him as she tossed wet paper towels in the garbage. "Root beer floats?"

"Now, that sounds perfect," Pops said. "Why didn't we think of that in the first place? We would have avoided all of this mess."

Steph laughed. "I'm glad we can all agree on the silver lining of this disaster."

"I don't see any disaster," Pops declared, his eyes twinkling.

She crossed to him and kissed his cheek. "You're right. Everything's just as it should be."

By the time they were on their way to the mountains where Brandy and Ian lived on adjacent properties, Pops had started complaining about a mysterious ache in his ankle.

"I wonder if I twisted something when I fell," he said, lifting his foot as if he could inspect it through his socks and tennis shoes.

"Possibly." Steph glanced over at him, then continued to watch the road, as she was driving this time. Cal had insisted on letting Pops sit in front. Steph wasn't surprised—she was definitely getting spoiled by this man. "When did it start hurting?"

"When I stubbed my toe and dropped the mixing bowl."

Steph met Cal's amused glance in the rearview mirror. "Hmm. If it still hurts tomorrow, we can call the doctor."

Instead of vehemently protesting like Steph expected him to, Pops said, "All right."

Just Add Friendship

She found herself smiling when Cal rested a hand on her shoulder and gave her a light squeeze.

They pulled in front of Brandy's place, which was a fixed-up cabin that had been in the Kane family for a while. Other cars lined the long driveway up to Ian's newer cabin.

"Wow, there are a lot of people here," Pops said.

"It just means more food choices," Steph said.

Cal helped Pops out of the car, and she noted again how nice it was to have him around. It was like her workload was cut in half, or almost felt nonexistent, because even if Cal hadn't been doing as much as he was, she enjoyed his presence.

"Food, right?" Pops said. "I'm starving."

"Really?" Steph asked with a laugh, linking arms with him.

Cal grabbed the box where they'd put in all the fixings for the root beer floats.

The closer they got to Ian's cabin, the louder the music and conversation grew. They found everyone in the back, where a barbecue was already cooking away on the deck.

A large golden retriever bounded toward them. Before he could plow into Pops, Steph reached out her hand. "Hey, Duke. How are you buddy?"

Duke sidled up to her and pressed against her leg as she gave him a rubdown.

Ian appeared. "Duke, come here. Let them settle in first." He strode toward them and took the box from Cal and peered inside. "What do we have here?"

"Dessert plan two," Cal said.

"Looks good to me."

"Ian, this is Cal Conner."

Ian nodded. He was olive-skinned like Cal, but had a leaner build, and his eyes were light green. "Great to meet you. Welcome. Have a seat anywhere and make yourselves comfortable."

As they moved farther into the yard, Steph introduced Cal to those he hadn't met. When he said he'd find Pops a seat and keep him company, Steph joined Brandy and Lori at the potluck table, where they were arranging the food. Julie wasn't there because she was staying home with her family, but Everly and Austin had shown up with his daughter, Jessica. Lydia had come with an older man Steph didn't recognize. He was about Lydia's height and had dark hair peppered with silver, which set off his copper skin tone. Was he a date?

"Who's your mom with?" she asked.

Brandy's eyes went comically wide. "He's from the senior group that she's been going to a few times a week. Name is Jorge."

"So he's from here?" Steph thought she knew most of the old-timers, but maybe not.

"He moved to Everly Falls last year to retire. Looking for small-town life, I guess. Lost his wife about a year ago."

"He looks like a nice guy," Steph said. "Not like that creeper Greg Makin."

"I like Jorge so far," Brandy said. "Although it is kind of weird for my mom to go from never dating to all of a sudden, she's looking."

"Not totally surprising, though," Lori said, her gaze turning to Steph. "She has a lot of vibrant years left—why spend them alone?"

"Why are you both looking at me like that?" Steph asked.

"How are we looking at Steph?" Everly asked, joining the group. Her sandy-blonde hair was tied back in a turquoise scarf that matched her flowy jumpsuit.

"They're talking about your mom's plus-one, but giving me the stare down."

"Oh, that's easy," Everly said, a smile growing on her face. "You show up with that hunk of a man while you keep telling all of us that you're just friends."

"We are friends."

"Not *just* friends, though," Lori said in a leading tone.

"Believe me, we've had *the talk*, and we're friends only." Steph knew her face was likely red. Brandy was the only one who knew about their kiss. Well, the first kiss. She didn't know about the second kiss in the parking lot after Julie's baby was born. "You guys know my record. In the past, I've jumped into things too fast. Cal's a friend, and it might have potential to change, but not for a long time. I'm trying the friendship thing first."

"Mm-hmm," Everly mused. "Well, since we're all together—I wanted to see who can come wedding dress shopping with me next weekend."

"What?" Lori said. "I thought you had your dress."

"I thought I did, too," Everly said with a scowl. "The wedding planner I was working with closed down her business suddenly. Just found out this morning. And she never put in the order for the dress with my requested alterations, so I'm out a dress, too."

Steph stared at Everly. "Are you serious?"

"Yep. So I'm starting from scratch, which means I have ten days to pull this thing off. I'm going to find a dress on Saturday and buy it off the rack."

"Oh, so sorry," Lori said with a grimace. "What a pain."

"Yeah, but we're just going to keep things super simple now," Everly said. "So maybe that will be better anyway. Who wants to come with me on Saturday?"

Steph wanted to go with her friends, but she didn't

know how work would play out this week with Pops's appointments. "I'll have to see how Pops is doing first. We're doing physical therapy this week, and I need to reschedule a bunch of my clients. What time are you thinking?"

Before Everly could answer, Brandy said, "Here's the thing, Steph. Cal told us all about your crazy schedule, and we're helping you this week. We're each taking a day to spend with Pops and take him where he needs to be. We've already decided on the rotation."

"What?" Steph stared at her. "You can't each take a day off from your jobs."

"You've got Monday," Brandy told her. "Lori's Tuesday, I'm on Wednesday, Everly is Thursday, and my mom is Friday. It's all worked out. You can get your time in at the salon. On Saturday, we'll go with Everly dress shopping while Cal takes that day with Pops."

Steph opened her mouth, then shut it. She looked over at Cal, who was sitting next to Pops. Austin was on their other side and his daughter stood in the mix of everyone, telling some story that was making them all laugh.

"When did Cal do this?" Steph asked.

"He texted us all this morning," Lori said.

Steph frowned, her mind trying to fit together the puzzle pieces. "How did he know your numbers?"

"He got mine when Julie was at the hospital, and it went from there." Brandy folded her arms, her smile growing. "He told us you might push back and try to cancel everything. So we're telling you that it's too late for that."

Steph didn't know if she was angry, annoyed, or impressed. "I need to talk to him." She strode away, making a beeline for Cal.

He looked up as she approached, and the smile dropped from his face. He quickly stood and stepped out of the group he was in. "Steph, you okay?" he asked in a quiet voice.

"We need to talk," she whispered.

His brows rose, but he didn't say anything more. He merely followed her around the side of the cabin, where no one could hear them.

Steph turned to face him, noting the concerned lines on his face. "My friends told me you recruited them to help with Pops. Cal, they can't take time off from their jobs. Pops is my responsibility, not theirs."

He didn't answer, just waited, because apparently he knew her well enough to know she wasn't finished talking.

"I knew what I was signing up for when I agreed to live with him," she continued. "My parents warned me, and I also talked to my boss Carol. I can't put my friends out, I can't." Steph's voice cut off, and she swallowed against the lump in her throat. Blinking rapidly against the burning in her eyes, she refused to cry.

Cal slipped his hands into his pockets. "Your friends want to help you, Steph. I didn't go begging. Brandy and Lori—and even Julie—repeatedly told me they want to help you, but that you never let them."

Steph rubbed the back of her neck because somehow she was aching there. "Everyone has their own lives, their own problems—I don't need to be a burden."

Cal reached for her hand. "You're far from a burden, Steph. Why is it okay that you help out your friends, but they can't help you? Isn't that what friendship is all about? Having each other's backs?"

Steph couldn't look at his imploring eyes, so she looked down at his hand holding hers.

"I don't know what in your life has made you feel like a burden, Bee," Cal said quietly. "Maybe it's the string of idiot men you've dated. Maybe it's the complication of Pops being a step-grandparent who your parents have left behind, and you feel like you have to make up for their behavior. Maybe it's other hurts that you've internalized . . . I really don't know. But I at least know one thing."

She was definitely crying now. She used her other hand to wipe away the renegade tears. "What?" she whispered.

"You deserve happiness, too," Cal said, his thumb moving over her knuckles. "You deserve as much love and fulfillment as everyone around you. I know you want the best for your friends, and it's natural they want the best for you, too. You need to stop pushing others away. Believe me, I know what it's like to go solo and how it fosters regret and loneliness. For all my father's faults, I waited much too long to reconcile."

Steph drew in a shaky breath and raised her gaze. Seeing moisture in Cal's eyes wasn't helping her keep her emotions under control. "I'm sorry about your father."

"I am, too," he said in a gentle tone. "But I can't go back in time and change things. You have the chance to change things now with your friends. Don't push them away. Let them help. Pops will enjoy it."

The tightness in her chest eased. "You're right, Pops will love all the attention, even if he acts grumpy about it."

Cal's smile appeared. "You know him so well."

A small laugh burst out of Steph. She stepped into Cal's arms, not sure if she was laughing or crying now. Even though she was grateful for her friends, it was still going to be hard to let them help. But if she could think of it as something Pops would love, that would make it easier.

Cal pulled her close and kissed the top of her head. She ignored the burst of butterflies in her stomach as she caught his scent. "My soap smells good on you."

He chuckled. "I like your soap."

It was a simple statement, in response to her own, yet it sent the butterflies tumbling again.

She drew away, because they'd been missing for way too long—and there was already enough speculation about her relationship with Cal.

"Thanks for being a friend."

He only smiled and squeezed her hand before releasing it. Something in her chest wanted him to keep ahold of her hand and never let go.

Twenty

CAL KNEW HE WAS IN love with Stephenie Grady, but as of now, she was the last person he'd tell. Which was ironic, since he had no one else to tell, so that meant no one would know. He hoped that might change someday, but she was keeping him quite firmly in the friend zone.

He didn't mind because he wanted to be around her—whatever form that took.

Okay, so he did mind. But he wasn't going to push her. He wasn't interested in becoming ghosted again.

It had been a week since the barbecue and a week since he'd seen her in person. But she'd been texting him regular updates on Pops, and a few times they texted about other things. Today, though, it was Cal's turn to watch over Pops while Steph spent a half day working, then the afternoon wedding dress shopping with Everly.

He hoped Steph would let herself have fun and not worry about anything. Strangely, he was also looking forward to hanging out with the old man. It seemed to fill a void he'd had with his dad, and he'd never known either of his grandparents.

The weather should be warm enough to hang out at the

park and have lunch there. Cal wanted to get Pops outside for a bit. A change of scenery and pace.

He left Grandin extra early so he could stop and pick up breakfast for everyone. He'd text Steph right before so that she didn't have time to protest. As he drove, his thoughts drifted to Aunt Rachel. He'd told her he'd be in town, but she was working this weekend and didn't need help with anything.

Cal decided he liked being needed, which was probably why he was always offering to help Steph and her grandpa. Living on his own and not having much family had made his world feel very small sometimes. But there was more . . . much more involving his feelings for Steph. He hadn't forgotten a thing about her in ten years, and he didn't want to be apart from her for even a few days. So the past week had been pretty much torture.

Once Cal arrived at Steph's home, he parked on the street and headed to the front door, bag of food in hand.

When Steph answered the door, she said, "You didn't have to bring breakfast," but she was smiling.

She was wearing a nut-brown dress that set off her red hair and made her blue eyes brilliant. She moved from the doorway, and he stepped inside. Pops was nowhere to be seen.

"Where is he?"

"Sleeping in," Steph said. "I checked on him a few minutes ago, and he's sawing away at a bunch of logs."

Cal chuckled. "Good for him. All that physical therapy this week must have worn him out. I'll take it easy on him today."

She touched his arm and stopped him before he could head into the kitchen. "Thanks again for coming, Cal. I think you're the one who Pops needs to take it easy on. Don't let him boss you around into doing chores."

Cal met her gaze. "Let me worry about that. You go ahead and enjoy your day."

She bit her lip, and he was almost positive she was going to say something more, but instead, she moved into the kitchen. "Breakfast smells good, what did you get?"

"Pancakes and hashbrowns. Also a fruit bowl."

Steph opened a cupboard and pulled down plates. "Sounds yummy. I packed a bagel since I don't get hungry this early in the morning."

"There will probably be leftovers if you want them later."

"That sounds good."

He watched her bring utensils to the table as he unloaded the food. "Everything all right?"

She paused. "Sure, why do you ask?"

He slipped his hands into his pockets. "You seem . . . I don't know. Like something's bothering you."

Her gaze assessed him. "I'm fine, but I guess I'm kind of jealous of Pops getting to spend the day with you. And not me."

Cal lifted his brows. "Really?"

She shrugged. "Really." She narrowed her eyes. "Why are you smiling?"

"I think that's the nicest thing you've ever said to me." He moved around the table to where she stood. "I could crash at Rachel's, and we could hang out tomorrow."

"Don't you have a job and a life to get back to?"

Cal smirked. "I have all of that, but I also have my priorities."

Steph set a hand on her hip. "I told you, no flirting."

"I'm speaking the truth, Bee," he said in a low voice. "How you choose to take it is on you, not me." Cal wanted to pull her close, lean in, and really flirt. Which of course included kissing.

But he'd promised to stay in the friend zone. Besides, Pops must have awakened, because a door shut, and a gravelly voice came from the hallway. "Dagnammit, where are my slippers?"

Without flinching or moving, Steph called out, "Next to your bedside table."

"Ah, found them!" Something banged. "Is that breakfast I smell?" Pops's voice grew closer. "So glad Cal is here today to put me to rights."

Steph smirked at Cal, and he chuckled.

"Well, have a nice day with Pops," she said, moving past Cal. Her shoulder bumped his, and he turned to watch her greet Pops as he arrived at the end of the hallway.

"Going so soon?" Pops said. "Cal just got here."

"Some of us have to work." Steph kissed his cheek. "Have a good day, but you'd better behave."

"You're always so bossy," Pops said. "Don't you think she's bossy, Cal?"

"Definitely." He flashed a smile at Steph, and she returned it.

As soon as she left, Pops shuffled over to the table. "Now what do we have here?"

"Eat up, Pops," Cal said. "We've got a full day ahead of us."

"Oh?" Pops settled into a chair. "Did you clear it with Steph?"

"Nope."

Pops chuckled. "Sounds perfect, then."

Cal grinned and dug into the food. His stomach had been grumbling for at least an hour, and he didn't know how Steph could ever skip breakfast. When his phone rang, he pulled it out of his pocket. He didn't recognize the number, so he sent it to voice mail. If it had to do with one of his clients, it could wait a little while.

Once Pops declared he was as full as a water buffalo, Cal cleaned up breakfast. "What do you need to do to get ready? Shower?"

"I showered up last night," Pops said. "I just need to get on my street clothes, then I'll be ready."

"Do you need help?"

"What do you think I am? An invalid?"

Cal opened his mouth to respond, but Pops waved him off. "I'll take care of all that. You be ready when I am."

"Great." His phone rang again.

"Better answer that or it'll be ringing all day." Pops headed down the hallway.

Cal pulled out the phone and answered.

"Is this Cal Conner?" the man on the other end asked.

"Sure is, what can I help you with?"

"This is Ian Hudson."

As in Brandy's boyfriend. But why in the world was he calling? "Oh, hey."

"I got your number from Brandy. So sorry to surprise you like this."

"It's fine. What's up?" Cal walked to the kitchen window to look out at the backyard, where the newly painted fence gleamed in the rising sun.

"Well, here's the thing," Ian said. "You know that Everly and Austin are getting married in about a week?"

"Yeah."

"It seems that everything they've booked through a wedding planner has now fallen apart. At first we thought the places were still booked even though the wedding planner copped out. We found out last night that nothing was ever booked."

"Oh wow. What are you going to do?"

"We're holding a backyard wedding at the Kanes'

Just Add Friendship

house." Ian paused. "Austin and I are going to take care of a few things ourselves today. We heard you're in town and wondered if you could help us out."

Cal's mind raced. He'd have to bring Pops along to whatever they had in mind. "What's the plan?"

"We're building a gazebo in the Kanes' backyard—where the marriage ceremony will take place," Ian said. "Austin and I will be picking up the lumber soon, but we'll need help with the construction if we want to get it done in one day."

"I have no problem with that," Cal said. "I should check with Pops first—see if he's up for this."

"Sure thing."

Cal headed down the hallway and tapped on Pops's bedroom door. It opened a moment later. Once he told him about the gazebo, the old man's eyes lit up. "Count me in. I'm a whiz at delegating to a crew of workers."

"He's in," Cal said into the phone to Ian. "What time should we meet you at the Kanes'?"

"About an hour?" he said. "We've also roped Lydia's new man, Jorge, into helping us. He's been a good sport about this, plus he's helping with Lydia's craft booth for the fall festival in a couple of weeks."

"Sounds like a good man," Cal said. "Pops and I will meet you in an hour."

Cal wondered if he should text Steph an update, but between getting Pops out of the house and a couple of surprise errands Pops wanted to do, which included buying his favorite brand of black licorice and grabbing a stack of newspapers, it all slipped his mind.

The day was busy, filled with work, laughter, and a couple breaks when Lydia brought out food and drinks for everyone.

"You men are lifesavers," she crooned, her adoring gaze on Jorge.

The man was talkative and friendly. His dark hair and complexion contrasted nicely with Lydia's blonde hair and lighter skin. Cal noticed them stealing a couple of moments away in private.

It was an interesting observation to see a widowed woman find love again. Cal had wondered more than once what might have happened if his dad had remarried. Would he have turned to such self-destruction and loneliness?

Pops was true to his word and sat in a padded lawn chair, reading aloud the newspaper headlines, and doling out helpful advice. Well, most of it was helpful. Apparently, he had worked in construction a number of summers as a younger man, so he did know what he was talking about.

Before Cal knew it, the day had sped by, the gazebo was up, and the painting had begun. With four men working, it was going by quickly. The sun was setting, splashing the sky with late September orange, when he heard the new arrivals.

Women's voices.

And that's when he remembered. He hadn't updated Steph on anything.

Twenty-one

STEPH COULD HARDLY BELIEVE THE news about Cal and Pops helping at the Kanes' house when Brandy told her what the men were up to. But when she hurried home after work to change before wedding dress shopping, Cal's car was gone, and the house was empty.

She'd sent him a text, just to confirm and make sure Pops was all right and not getting too tired out. But that had been three hours ago, and she hadn't received any reply from Cal.

While Everly tried on white dress after white dress, Steph wondered if she was obsessed with worrying. One side of her brain was telling her that Cal and Pops were perfectly fine. If there was some issue, then Cal would call her. He was probably caught up in the gazebo work and wasn't checking his phone.

Pops was likely having the time of his life.

There was nothing to worry about, right?

Steph should be able to relax, enjoy the time with her friends as Everly picked out a gorgeous wedding dress. What was there to stress about?

But her thoughts had continued to race and jump to all

sorts of conclusions. Somehow, though, she managed to smile and banter her way through the afternoon, and no one seemed to notice that she felt panicky inside.

So it wasn't until Steph walked into the Kanes' backyard and physically saw Pops sitting in a lawn chair, a bottle of juice in his hand, and Cal crouching at the base of the gazebo, adding a layer of paint, did she finally breathe easy. That, and berate herself for spending the last few hours on pins and needles. Worrying. Needlessly.

"How did it go, ladies?" Lydia rose from the chair she sat in. "Find something?"

"I did," Everly said with a broad smile. "I think I like it better than the original one I had picked out."

Austin was already heading toward his bride-to-be, and Steph watched as he pulled her close and kissed her.

Everly drew back, smiling. "About done with the gazebo? We should pick up Jessica from her friend's."

"Oh, I forgot to tell you," he said. "Jessica asked to sleep over, so it's just us tonight."

They shared another smile, and Steph had to look away. The next scene wasn't much better because Brandy was glued to Ian, laughing at something he was talking about.

Jorge had grabbed a drink, and Lydia stood close to him, her hand on his arm.

In this backyard, Steph was surrounded by sappiness. Well, love, and friends . . . but sappy all the same. There was only one thing left to do. She crossed to where Cal had straightened from his painting. The gazebo gleamed white against the background of trees bursting with red, orange, and yellow autumn leaves.

He was the best view of all, though. He wasn't wearing the jacket he'd arrived in. His gray fitted T-shirt had a few paint splotches on it. His dark hair had some paint flecks, and there was a smudge of white paint on his collarbone. In short, he looked like a man who'd put in a hard day's work, but was happy about it.

"Looks like you've had a busy day," she said, keeping her voice casual. "Pops keeping you all in line?"

Cal smiled. "Something like that. Hey, sorry I didn't let you know—things happened kind of fast."

Steph waved a hand as if that was all it took to make up for her hours of persistent worry. "It's fine. Everly told us what was going on. I only hoped Pops could make it through the day all right."

Cal glanced over at the man, who was entertaining Jorge with some story. "He's been fine. I offered to take him home for a break a couple different times, but he kept refusing."

"Not surprised." She reached for the paintbrush Cal held and stepped closer to the gazebo.

"Aren't you worried about your dress?" he asked, folding his arms.

"It's only a couple of touch-ups."

Cal watched her for a moment, then said, "Everything went all right?"

"Yeah," Steph answered.

"But...?"

She looked over to see his brown eyes steady on hers. How did he know? Somehow he always knew when she was holding something back. "Watching someone try on dresses for three hours isn't really my thing. I'm more of an in-and-out shopper. Or online, I guess. If I like it and it's on a good sale, I grab it. Then leave."

Cal's eyes crinkled with his smile. "I think a three-hour fitting would drive me nuts, too."

"I've already decided that if I ever get married, I'll just borrow Everly's dress. It's very pretty, and we're about the same size."

His brows tugged together. "You're not the same size."

Steph blinked. "What are you talking about? We're both the same height and not too skinny."

"Uh . . ." Cal's gaze moved over her. Down to her feet, then up again.

She willed her face not to turn red. "Are you checking me out?"

"I am," he said in a low voice. "But only to verify that you could not wear Everly's wedding dress."

Steph handed back the paintbrush. "Because I'm fatter than her?"

He didn't even flinch. "Because you're curvier, and classier. Different types and styles."

She stared at him for a moment. "What are you? Some sort of fashion expert?"

"Not at all." He had the good sense to flush a little, but his gaze remained steady. "I just know what you look like compared to other women." He moved closer, invading most of her space.

But she held her ground.

"You're beautiful, Bee," Cal said. "I can tell my friend that, right? Because honesty is important in friendships. Besides, every woman deserves her own wedding dress."

Steph had no words. She hadn't known Cal was so sentimental. He was also willing to put in a full day's labor for one of *her* friends. In addition to watching over *her* grandpa. What else would she learn about him before the day was up?

"Should I order pizza?" Lydia said somewhere in the background.

But Steph was still watching Cal. "Are you flirting with me?"

"No, I'm speaking the truth." He touched the brush to the gazebo and painted over a streak. "Take it how you will."

Just Add Friendship

Steph watched him paint for a few more minutes, touching up here and there. The conversations around the yard had become indistinguishable buzzing. All she could focus on was Cal. They weren't speaking, but they didn't need to. Steph felt comfortable enough with him to be around him and not talk. Not fill the silence with mindless chatter.

"See any other spots that need attention?" he asked after several moments.

Steph moved her gaze to the gazebo. "I don't. It's all excellent for a single day's work."

He set the paintbrush down and turned toward her. "So, I had a client call earlier today, and I have a job that will run all next week and probably into the weekend."

Steph nodded, thinking immediately how that meant she wouldn't see him for a while. "Sounds important."

"Yeah." Cal looked past her, then met her gaze. "The guys sort of invited me to the wedding—nothing official, of course. But I'm not going to jump in the middle of your thing."

"It's fine with me, if that's what you're asking. I'll be there as a bridesmaid, and it would be fun to see you." Steph was surprised, but she wasn't surprised. Cal had gotten to know Ian and Austin today. She'd invited him to the barbecue last weekend. Cal might be considering her friends his friends now. She'd analyze how she felt about that later.

"Great," he said, his expression brightening. "I should be able to make it. The job will be wrapped up by then."

Steph nodded, her mind going to what Cal looked like dressed up in a suit. She had no complaints about him completely casual, of course.

He was still watching her—what else did he want to say? What he asked next could not have been predicted.

"Are you bringing a date?"

"What? No . . ." She felt her neck heat. In seconds, she'd be blushing. "I'm not dating anyone. You know that."

Cal nodded, the edge of his mouth lifting. "Just checking."

Then her stomach felt like it dropped a foot. "Why, are you bringing a date? I'm sure it would be fine with Everly and Austin."

He tilted his head. "Are you blushing?"

"No," she said immediately, maybe too fast.

"I'm not bringing a date, Steph," Cal said. "Unless you want to be my date, but I already know the answer."

She opened her mouth, then wisely closed it.

"Maybe I can bring Pops if you're busy doing . . ." He waved a hand. "Bridesmaid stuff."

Steph blinked. Sometimes she wanted to stomp on Cal's foot for being such a great guy. How was he so great and still single?

"How about we cross that bridge later?" she said, because she was feeling overwhelmed now. "There's a lot of changes happening, but I don't know the exact details of the wedding day."

"Fair enough," Cal said stiffly, and moved to pick up the paint cans.

Steph wondered if she'd said something wrong. Couldn't he just be a guest at the wedding? Did he always have to be Mr. Helpful? "Thanks for helping out my friends today," she said, hoping to see his smile, or something more.

He merely nodded. "No problem." Then he moved past her, carrying the paint cans.

Steph watched him walk away. What was going on? Should she follow him?

Just then, the pizza arrived, and everyone busied themselves with arranging food, pouring drinks, and eating.

Cal returned and sat by Pops after fetching him a plate of pizza. Steph had planned to do the same, but now Cal was there. So she sat on the other side of Pops and listened with half an ear to her friends talking about the bridal shower, while trying to follow Cal and Pops talking about tonight's baseball game.

Steph wanted to jump in and ask Cal if he'd come over and watch the game. Maybe he would stay overnight at Rachel's like he'd suggested earlier, and tomorrow they could do something. What, she didn't know... And what was she thinking? Asking him on a date? When she'd so firmly friend-zoned him?

She was tired, that was all. From stressing all day about Pops—well, all week, to be exact. From having so many moving parts in her life with friends, work, and the adjusted wedding plans. Why should *she* be so stressed, though? Everly should be the one wigging out. But she sat close to Austin, hand in hand, as they joked together.

Steph's gaze slid once more to Cal. Maybe he really did like hanging out with Pops. They were like bosom buddies. Maybe with her out of the picture, Cal would still come around to help Pops.

No...

She bit her lip and looked away from Cal's brown eyes, handsome face, and easygoing manner. She couldn't let herself get too attached to him, become dependent on him. It was how all those other men duped her. She didn't want Cal to disappear. Not even for a week. But there was nothing she could do about that. It was his job, after all... and when this job was done, there'd be another.

And she was fine with that. It wasn't like they were dating or anything. Missing him as a friend was much easier than missing him if they were something more. Which they weren't.

After the pizza, and after cleanup, Steph told Cal, "I can take Pops home if you need to get on the road."

He gazed at her for a heartbeat, then two. "If you're sure?"

"I'm sure." She wasn't sure, and the words tasted sour in her mouth. "Unless you really wanted to watch the game with him?" *Or stay overnight?*

"I think he's going to be falling asleep in front of that game."

Steph smiled a smile she didn't feel. "True. He's had quite the day."

"I'm not getting any younger," Pops said, coming around the corner on Brandy's arm. "Cal, got your car warmed up?"

"I'm taking you, Pops, so Cal can get on the road." Steph wanted to kick herself the second the words were out. She should have let Cal answer, because maybe it would have been different.

Pops's step slowed, and he released Brandy's arm. "Are you two fighting again?"

"No one's fighting." Steph's cheeks were blazing. "Cal's been here all day, doing double-duty, that's all." She peeked over at him.

He simply stood there, hands in his pockets, his dark eyes on her. Letting her take the heat.

"Come on." She stepped forward and took Pops's arm. "What time does the game start?"

But he shook her off. "I need to speak to Cal, man-to-man, then I'll meet you at your car."

Nothing could have surprised Steph more. "What about?" she asked before she could stop herself.

"Never you mind."

She held back a frustrated sigh. She glanced at Brandy, who shrugged.

Just Add Friendship

"All right," Steph said. Now, she had no choice but to head to her car, with Brandy right behind her.

"Everything okay?" Brandy asked quietly.

"Pops gets cranky sometimes," Steph said. "I don't think he's too happy about Cal leaving, but the guy has been here all day and then some. He's always doing us favors, and I can't return them—" Her voice choked off, and she hated that her eyes were burning with tears.

At least she'd reached her car and could hide there until Pops deigned to show up.

"Hey," Brandy said in a gentle tone, grasping her arm. "You okay? What's going on?"

Steph took a shuddering breath, then turned to her friend. The kindness in Brandy's blue eyes was her undoing.

"I really like him, Brandy," she whispered. "More than like him. I . . . I don't want to mess this up like I've messed up all my other relationships."

Brandy's eyes widened. "Why do you think you'd mess things up with Cal? He's totally into you, Steph. You can't say you haven't noticed."

"I've noticed he really like Pops," she said. "It might sound petty to say this, but Cal sees him as the father figure he's never had."

Brandy took a step closer. "Cal's not coming around because of your grandpa. Give the man more credit. He's coming around because he wants out of the friend zone, and he's being extremely patient, if you ask me."

Steph released a sigh. "Whether he likes me or not isn't the question. Because I'm terrible at relationships, and I'd rather have him as a friend than as a nothing."

"I get that you don't want to date him because you think it will only end in disaster," Brandy said. "But what you don't have is another Cal."

"What do you mean?"

"I mean," Brandy lowered her voice because Pops was now heading their way, "none of those men you dated were Cal. He's the real deal, and I think that's why you're scared."

Steph was scared, she couldn't deny that. Scared of giving a man her heart and having it rejected. Especially when that man was Cal. He would be impossible to recover from.

"Thanks, Brandy," Steph said, because Pops was now within hearing distance. She gave her friend a quick hug, then released her. She didn't know where Cal was, but Pops was already climbing in her car, so she climbed in, too.

As they pulled away from the curb, Steph said in a cheerful tone, "You had a busy day."

"I'm going to tell you this once, and I hope you remember it, Steph. Great men don't grow on trees."

Twenty-two

STEPH REREAD THE TEXTS SHE and Cal had exchanged in the last couple of days as she sat in her car, right before heading back into the Kanes' house. The wedding would start in a couple of hours, and she'd be helping the other bridesmaids finish last-minute details for the bride.

But right now, her mind wasn't on the wedding, but Cal. His job had ended last Saturday, but he'd made no gesture to come to Everly Falls. And with all the wedding planning, she didn't have time to visit Grandin. Plus, she didn't want to be an hour away from Pops in the foreseeable future.

He was still doing physical therapy, and her friends had been generous to help with his appointments this past week. So Steph felt okay about leaving him home when she was working, although she'd bought him a medical alert bracelet to notify the paramedics if he fell.

The text exchanges with Cal had been casual, almost superficial. He hadn't renewed his offer about taking Pops to the wedding, and Steph didn't know what she would have done if he had. So she'd brought Pops along with her, and he was parked in the living room of the Kane house, chatting with Jorge.

Steph had returned to her car because she needed privacy, and she didn't want anyone to overhear her phone call to Cal. She knew if she didn't do it now, she'd chicken out again. Whether he was coming or not . . . she needed to tell him. Several chats with Brandy had convinced Steph that if she never took a chance, then she might as well give up Cal completely.

And she couldn't do that. At least not without her confession.

Oh, and Pops's berating had only solidified that Steph was being very, very obtuse.

Cal Conner did like her, and he deserved to know how she felt about him. She only hoped he hadn't changed his mind about her.

Steph drew in a breath, closed her eyes for a few seconds, then opened them. She was ready. For better or for worse.

She called his number, not knowing if he'd answer. He could be driving to Everly Falls right now. Or maybe he wasn't coming to the wedding. She hadn't dared to ask him or presume. And she hadn't dared to ask Austin or Ian about him either.

The phone rang four times, then went to voice mail, which told her at least he wasn't screening her calls. As his voice message came on, her heart thumped loudly. The phone beeped, and the moment arrived.

"Hey, Cal," she said, knowing she sounded breathless, but it was too late to hang up now. "I wasn't sure if you were coming to Everly and Austin's wedding, but I wanted you to know . . ." She paused. "I wanted you to know that I'm really grateful for all your help these past few weeks. Pops has turned a corner in so many ways, and I know it's because of your relationship with him. But I also wanted to say that I'm grateful to have you in my life, too." This was where the words began to waver because she couldn't keep the emotion out of her voice. "I know I told you we needed to just be friends because I'm terrible at relationships beyond friendship . . . but I wondered what you'd think if I changed my mind."

She paused to catch her breath over her wildly beating heart. "I guess it's not really changing my mind about *you*, because you're an amazing man, and I've known that for a long time. Ten years, to be exact. It's changing my mind about our *situation*. I just . . . I just wanted to tell you that I've seen the light, so to speak, and I . . . miss you. And I'm sorry if I've said or done things that made you think I don't like you. Because I do like you. I mean, you already know that, but you also know how messy I can make things when dating a guy . . . but I guess I wanted to know if you don't mind a little messy. Then maybe—"

There was a beep and the call cut off.

Steph stared at the phone in disbelief. Her message was so long and rambling that the voice mail had decided it was enough. Her stomach twisted. Should she call back? Leave a second message?

She needed advice, but she couldn't burst into the house and talk to Brandy, who was helping her sister get ready for her wedding. Steph closed her eyes and reviewed what she'd said. She'd made herself clear. A second voice mail wouldn't change or redeem anything.

If Cal thought she was ridiculous, then so be it. She'd just have to break the news gently to Pops later on that he wouldn't be coming around anymore.

A text beeped on her phone, and her heart nearly stopped.

But it was the friend group chat, with Julie saying she was on her way. Dave would bring the kids over later.

Steph climbed out of the car so that when Julie arrived, she wouldn't question why Steph was hiding out there. Once inside the house, it wasn't hard to find the women gathered in the master bedroom, getting ready for the big event.

No one seemed to realize that Steph had arrived earlier, dropped Pops off in the living room, then gone back to her car. But she did feel Brandy's eyes on her more than once. Steph had told her that if Cal came tonight, she was going to talk to him. The phone call was to get it mostly out of the way—they'd still need to talk, but at least Steph had broken the ice with saying some of her piece.

"Sorry I'm late, everyone," Julie said, bursting into the room. "I had a little trouble with my girdle."

"We could have helped you," Brandy said, and everyone laughed.

They were all wearing the same deep blue color, but in different dress styles. At least the bridesmaid dresses hadn't been messed up because everyone bought their own. Steph's dress was form-fitting satin, with a V-neck and three-quarter-length sleeves. She'd pinned up her hair, and wore silver jewelry.

"Let's get you in the wedding dress, then do the hair and makeup." Brandy moved to the closet and drew out the gown. The white silk glimmered in the afternoon light coming through the windows.

"You're going to look amazing," Lori gushed.

"Truly," Steph added, trying to focus on the event at hand and not wanting to check her phone. It was in her purse on the other side of the room. Would she hear an incoming text? She'd turned up the volume on high.

As they readied Everly, Steph discreetly checked it a couple of times, but no reply arrived from Cal.

It was fine, she told herself. He was probably driving.

Just Add Friendship

Or hadn't listened to her message yet.

Or was coming up with a plan to turn her down gently.

Another hour passed, and Everly was ready—primped and preened and sculpted and painted—glowing like she deserved.

"Can I see her?" a young voice asked from the hallway. It must be Austin's daughter, Jessica.

"I'll ask," Lydia said from outside. She tapped on the door and opened it. "Oh wow, you're gorgeous, darling." She stepped into the room with Jessica trailing behind, wide-eyed. "Jessica wants to see the dress."

"Of course." Everly turned from the full-length mirror with a smile. "Come here, I'll show you the bouquet, too."

Jessica beamed and moved toward her soon-to-be stepmother.

As Jessica asked questions in excited tones, Steph moved to her purse again and took out her phone. Nothing. She exhaled slowly. She needed to focus on Everly and the important day. Not on Cal's reaction to her voice mail.

She put the phone on silent, then put it back into her purse. Next she slipped out of the room to check on Pops. He wasn't in the living room, it turned out, but in the backyard, seated in one of the rows. Several wedding guests had already arrived, and it looked like Austin's dad was chatting with Pops.

He seemed to be in good hands.

When Steph returned to the master bedroom, Everly stood with her bouquet, ready. Lori was snapping some selfies, so Steph joined in, putting on a bright smile.

Time zoomed by after that, and when Austin's father, Mr. Hayes, came to fetch Everly, everything suddenly became real. Brandy ushered Jessica to the backyard, where she would walk down the aisle as the flower girl. The music started up, soaring through the yard, and Steph's heart soared right along with it.

Whatever happened tonight, whatever took place between her and Cal, right now, she was happy for Everly and Austin.

After Jessica, Brandy walked down the aisle, arm in arm with Ian.

Steph was paired up with one of Austin's friends from out of town. The blond man, Brad, gave her a cheesy grin, and she smiled back, but only briefly. She wasn't here to make new friends.

As she began to walk, she glanced over at Pops, half hoping that Cal had slipped in without her seeing him. But someone else was sitting by Pops, who nodded and winked at her. She winked back, not sure what the winking was all about, but she'd play along.

Once all the bridesmaids and groomsmen were in place, Everly came down the aisle on the arm of her soon-to-be father-in-law. She looked radiant in her off-the-shoulder dress, which fanned into a beautiful train.

Steph blinked at the stinging in her eyes, witnessing Austin's first look at Everly in her wedding dress. As a couple, they'd been through plenty of ups and downs, but their good hearts had won out.

Steph wiped at a tear before the vows started, and she couldn't look at the couple's faces, or else the tears would continue. Instead, she focused on sweet Jessica.

The rings were exchanged, then Austin pulled Everly close and kissed her soundly. Everyone clapped and cheered, and the congratulations began. Steph was pulled into a few photos with the bridesmaids and Everly, then a larger bridal group with various cousins. She made a quick check of her phone—still nothing—then she headed to where Pops was still seated, now by himself.

"You hungry?" she asked. "The buffet should start soon."

"I'm hungry, but I can wait," Pops said. "You enjoy yourself with your friends."

Brandy arrived at Steph's side and linked arms. "Let's go make some song requests for the dancing."

"Put in some oldies for me," Pops said. "None of that hip-hop stuff. Makes my old bones rattle just listening to it."

Brandy laughed. "Look at you, Pops, knowing music genres."

His ears pinked, but he was smiling.

"Come on, Brandy," Steph said, tugging her away. "I'm sure we can talk the DJ into playing a couple of oldies."

They threaded their way through the gathering and approached the man with spiky bleach-blond hair, as if he were trying to keep the eighties alive all by himself. He was currently playing mellow music while people mingled and formed a line at the buffet tables.

"What can I help you with, ladies?" the man asked.

Brandy gave him a list of songs, then Steph said, "We'd also love a song that would appeal to our older guests."

"Sure thing," the DJ said with a lopsided grin. "I've got just the thing."

"Excellent." Brandy detoured Steph away from the tables and the main crowd. "So, tell me what's up."

It took Steph a second to realize what she might be referring to. "What are you talking about?"

"Don't even play coy with me, *Bee*."

It was official, Steph was being called out. Brandy was the only one who knew about Cal's nickname for her.

"Before the wedding started, I left a message on his phone," Steph said quickly before she lost her nerve.

"And . . . what did you say?" Brandy asked.

Steph drew in a deep breath. "I told him I like him and

want him out of the friend zone, although I rambled a lot more than that." She winced. "He hasn't responded at all, and he hasn't shown up to the wedding."

Brandy smiled. "I'm so proud of you."

"Well, you're the only one, because I think I totally embarrassed myself," Steph said. "But it wouldn't be the first time."

"If he's the man I think he is, he'll show up and sweep you off your feet."

"Ha ha." Steph set her hands on her hips. "He wouldn't even have to do any sweeping, but I'm pretty sure I'll be solo the rest of the night. Well, except for Pops."

Brandy laughed. "Pops is the best."

"He is, but not really the same."

Brandy stepped close and hugged Steph. "Hang in there."

"Thanks," she murmured. She might cry about all of this later, but right now, she was going to eat and dance and have fun.

Once she and Pops ate, she got him to dance to one number. He then begged off and said he wanted to sit and watch. But Steph spied him dancing with Lydia Kane at one point, both of them all smiles. It was sweet, really. And it was neat to see Lydia enjoying her time with Jorge, too.

"Wanna dance, pretty lady?" Brad the groomsman asked, coming to stand next to her.

She didn't love the endearment, but the guy seemed harmless. "Sure."

They danced, and Brad kept trying to spin her in some complicated twirl, until Steph finally said, "Thanks so much. I'm parched, so I'll see you a little later."

It didn't take long for him to find another dancing partner.

She headed to get a drink, and when she finished, she

stood outside the main dancing area, watching. The sun had set, and the lights strung about the yard glowed against the twilight sky, making everything feel magical and dreamlike.

Everly and Austin danced several times together, then with other people as well, including little Jessica. The DJ switched to slower songs, and couples formed across the dance space. Maybe Steph should sit with Pops. Get off her feet and keep him company.

Before she could turn away from the dancing couples, an arm slipped around her waist and turned her inward. She was too startled to react at first. Looking up, she gazed into familiar brown eyes.

"Cal."

"Sorry I'm late."

Goose bumps raced across her skin, and her heart felt like it had flown away. Cal wore a full suit—the most formal she'd ever seen him—and her expectations were more than met. Suits definitely worked for this man. He drew her closer, and somehow, she was dancing with Cal, his hands at her waist, her hands at his shoulders.

They moved slowly to the music, and a dozen questions went through Steph's mind. Why was he so late? Had he gotten her message? What did he think?

Well, it was obvious he wasn't annoyed too much, because he was holding her rather close and pretty much staring at her.

"Were you working?" she asked.

"There was a huge accident, and both sides of the highway were closed for a couple of hours."

"Oh, that's terrible."

He nodded, but only kept gazing at her.

"You're staring," she finally said.

"I'm trying to read your mind."

He said it with such seriousness that she laughed, which

might have something to do with her jumping nerves. "You can ask me any questions, you know."

He leaned close and spoke low against her ear. "Was your voice mail the real deal?"

Her skin buzzed with warmth. "Yes," she whispered.

"Every word?"

"Yes."

Somehow he'd maneuvered them to the edge of the dancing, so it didn't take long for him to lead her around the gazebo, out of sight of everyone. He pulled her to a stop, his hand still holding hers. "So I'm out of the friend zone?"

Steph's pulse hammered. The twilight sky made his eyes seem even darker, and his white shirt collar a stark contrast to his olive skin. "Yes, if you want to be out of the friend zone. I mean, I'm not going to presume—"

Before she could finish, his hands cradled her face and his mouth found hers.

Her breath fled her body for an instant, but then she was kissing him back. His hands slipped behind her neck, then down her back, creating a rippling sensation. Her heels lifted from the ground as he drew her tightly against him, and every part of her body heated in response.

He wasn't changing his mind or rejecting her offer.

He was here, solid, real, living, breathing, and kissing her like she meant something to him. She locked her arms around his neck because she was pretty sure she was about to float away.

His mouth moved along her jaw, then to her neck, and she closed her eyes, letting the sensation of his touch and taste take over all of her senses. Somewhere in the background, music played, and people chattered, but it all felt so far away. Steph only wanted to focus on the here and now, and the man who held her in his arms.

Twenty-three

THE SILK OF STEPH'S DRESS gleamed silver in the moonlight, and she looked absolutely ethereal. Cal had spotted her at once when he'd joined the wedding celebration. He'd watched her for a few moments from the other side of the yard. Getting here had been aggravating to say the least, but he'd listened to her voice mail several times. Maybe even a dozen times. And he wasn't going to turn around no matter how many hours the road was closed.

So it was fortunate to arrive before the wedding was over, and now that he'd made it clear that he was accepting her offer to get out of the friend zone, he knew it was time to return to the wedding festivities. The DJ had just said something about the cake cutting. And he overheard a woman say, "Where's Steph? Has anyone seen her?"

"Bee," he whispered against her ear as her rapid breathing matched his. He probably had her lipstick on his collar, but he didn't care. Being able to hold her, to kiss her, to just be with her, felt like living inside his best dream. "They're cutting the cake."

"Mmm." Her arms tightened about him, making him smile.

"Are your bridesmaid duties done for the night?" he rasped. "As much as I like hiding out behind the gazebo, we could get out of here."

He felt her smile against his skin, then she drew away and gazed at him.

He liked what he saw—no, he loved it. Steph's eyes bright, skin flushed, lips swollen because she'd been thoroughly kissed... by him.

She blinked, then smiled. "You're right, I need to be at the cake cutting, because then they're throwing the bouquet."

He loved her smile.

"How's my hair?" She reached up to touch it.

He scanned her appearance. She looked beautifully disheveled. One of her dress straps had slipped, and her updo was a lot looser than he remembered. He moved her strap up on her shoulder, then skimmed his fingers down her arm, and linked their hands. "You look perfect."

"Well," she said in a breathless voice, "at least it's dark now, and the lights will hide a lot."

Cal wasn't sure about that, but he'd go along with it. Before they could walk around the gazebo and join the wedding party, Steph stopped him by putting her hand at his waist.

"Wait," she said. "You never really answered my question."

"What? You need words?"

The edge of her mouth lifted. "Please."

"Okay, then." He squeezed her hand. "We're definitely not just friends anymore, Stephenie Grady. We're officially dating."

"Okay." She grinned, then rose up to kiss him again.

He had to keep it brief, or it wouldn't be brief at all, but kissing her was easily his favorite activity of all time. "Ready?"

"Yes."

"We're holding hands?" He had to ask.

"Of course."

Well, he could live with that. And his long drive over had given him a lot of things to think about, namely that he didn't like living an hour from Steph. The more he thought about it, the more he realized that nothing was keeping him in Grandin, but there were a lot of things to draw him to Everly Falls.

He didn't want to jump ahead too fast, but he knew what he wanted . . . or more specifically, who he wanted. He supposed he had for a decade.

She led him around the gazebo, and surprisingly, his pulse hammered with nerves. Being seen as a couple with Steph was like entering into her life, more than just an occasional friend or sidekick. Her friends would be his friends. Her world would become his world. Pops would be . . . almost family . . .

The old guy was standing with Lydia and Jorge as the DJ told everyone to gather around for the cake cutting.

"There you are." Brandy's smile was huge. Right behind her walked Ian. Her eyes flicked over them, not missing the handholding. "It's almost time for the bouquet toss and you need to be there with me."

Steph laughed. "All right. Fine. I'll come with you when it happens."

Ian and Brandy stood by them, holding hands, and chatting about some of the wedding guests, while everyone jostled for position to see the cake cutting.

Steph kept ahold of Cal's hand. He had no problem with that.

"I'm glad you came tonight, Cal," she murmured.

"Me too." He smiled down at her, tempted to kiss her

again in this very public setting, when someone shouted, "Hooray!"

Others took up the cheer, and Brandy grabbed Steph's arm. "Come on, or we'll miss it."

The two women took off through the crowd to join the gathering of young women ready to catch the bouquet.

"Funny tradition," Cal said to Ian, but then he realized Ian wasn't standing next to him anymore. Interesting.

The crowd had parted to create a thoroughfare for the bouquet toss. Cal watched Brandy and Steph teasing and elbowing each other. Up ahead of them, Everly held the bouquet, wearing a huge grin.

The DJ played a countdown tune, and the crowd joined in. When the number got to three, Everly turned her back to everyone and tossed the bouquet backward over her head. The bouquet made a neat arc, and several women scrambled to catch it.

Steph stepped out of the way just as Brandy leapt to snag it. She squealed and held it up triumphantly. Everyone started clapping, and Everly walked over to hug her sister.

Then, as the sisters released each other, Brandy turned back to the crowd. She grinned at Ian, who was apparently standing on the side, not too far away.

He stepped out of the crowd and knelt in front of her.

The music quieted, as if Ian had tipped off the DJ. When her eyes widened, almost comically, everyone shushed each other.

Cal's heart thumped. Ian was going to propose. Right here, right now.

"Brandy Kane," he said, his voice quiet, but clear enough for everyone to hear. "I know this might be a surprise, but I can't wait another day. Or night." He shrugged.

Brandy brought her hand to her mouth, and her eyes swam with tears. "Ian . . ." she whispered.

"I thought you might want to tell your sister the good news, if there will be good news, before she disappears on her honeymoon for a week."

A few laughs scattered through the crowd.

"I love you with all that I have," Ian said. "You are my everything, and I don't want to wait any longer to tell you that you're the most important thing in my life. Will you do me the honor of becoming my wife? Any day you choose is fine with me."

Brandy lowered her hand and wiped at the tears on her cheeks. "Ian, we haven't even talked about this."

"We can start tonight," he said in a hopeful tone. "I don't have a ring yet because I knew you'd want to pick out your own."

Brandy nodded as if she was happy about his choice.

Cal held back a laugh because it was pretty clear that she would be saying yes. She was just getting over her surprise on the timing.

"Okay," Brandy said in a rush. "I'll marry you." She closed the distance between them, and Ian rose and scooped her into his arms.

Everyone cheered and people started patting Ian on his back, although he wasn't paying much attention because he was busy kissing his new fiancé.

Cal clapped along with everyone else, his heart more than full. Brandy and Ian made a great pair, and he wished them all the best. He headed toward the couple and congratulated them both. Then Jorge grabbed him. "You made it. Good to see you."

"Got stuck in the traffic from an accident," Cal said. "Glad I could make it, too."

They chatted for a minute, then Austin joined them. "Thanks for coming, Cal. Means a lot."

"No problem," Cal said. "Sorry I missed the ceremony. Looks like everything went well?"

"It all went great, but I guess I'm now waiting on my bride to celebrate with her sister." He laughed. "I should have known Ian was up to something. He's been quiet all day."

Cal didn't exactly see Ian as the talkative type anyway, but Austin knew the guy a lot better than he did. "Your wedding day will have even more memories now."

"Yeah." Austin chuckled. "Well, when we get back, we'll have to get together for dinner or something."

"Sure thing."

When Austin moved on, Cal scanned the crowd for Steph, because suddenly he wanted to see her. Needed to see her. Needed to be with her. All this sappy happiness and celebrating made him want to be with the one woman he knew he was in love with.

He spotted her by the cake, surrounded by Julie and Lori, but Steph was looking right at him. And smiling.

His heart jolted, and he smiled back.

Then they were both walking toward each other, threading their way through the crowd that was still congratulating Brandy and Ian, with Everly and Austin in the midst of everyone.

When Cal finally reached Steph, she stopped before he could grab her hand or hug her or kiss her. "I'm ready to go home," she said, tilting her head, her eyes sparkling. "You coming?"

"Of course."

She smirked, then slipped her hand in his. They walked together to find Pops.

"It's about time you noticed I'm over here wasting away," Pops said. "I almost had to ask Lydia Kane if I could borrow her couch for the night."

"Oh, Pops, you've been living it up." Steph linked her arm through his. "Cal's coming home with us, so you need to behave yourself."

Pops looked over at him, noticing how Steph held his hand. "It's about time you talked some sense into her. I see you're sticking together, now."

"That's right," Cal said. "Your granddaughter has finally seen reason."

"Funny," she said, but she squeezed his hand.

Cal decided that splitting up from Steph to drive his car over to her house was nearly torture. He didn't want to be separated from her quite yet. But he resolutely headed to his car. He sent a quick text to Rachel to see if he could spend the night at her place. He wasn't sure if she was working, but he hoped to talk to her at some point about the plans he wanted to make.

Plans that would only happen if Steph was good with them, too.

By the time he reached Steph's house, Rachel had texted back that he was fine to stay at her place, and she'd be happy to see him. Cal texted back a thanks, then climbed out of the car.

He jogged to where Steph was escorting Pops into the house. Cal took his other arm, and they all headed inside together.

"Boy, am I tired," Pops said. "I think I'll head to bed right now. You two enjoy yourselves."

Cal looked over at Steph as Pops headed down the hallway.

"What did you say?" he whispered.

"I didn't have to say anything." She walked toward him. "He did all the talking anyway, and I could only nod and agree with him."

"What did you agree with?"

"That you're an amazing guy and that I'm a stubborn woman."

Cal smiled. "Well, I can agree with that."

"Ha." She shoved at his arm, and he caught her hand, then brought it to his lips. "You smell like cake. How come I didn't get any?"

"I guess you were busy?" she said, looping her arms around his neck.

Cal could get used to this—very quickly. "What are your plans tomorrow?"

"Sleeping in, then working in the afternoon." She wrinkled her nose. "I should warn you, I'm kind of a boring person."

"You're far from boring, Bee." He leaned down and kissed her softly. "I'm going to be hanging around for a day or two, staying at Rachel's. Want me to bring over dinner?"

Steph bit her lip. "No. Let's go somewhere to eat. Lydia and Jorge told me they wanted to come visit Pops tomorrow night anyway. Play some new board game together." She nestled closer to him. "Then we can see if we still like each other without Pops around."

Cal smirked. "I hope you're not serious, because liking you has nothing to do with your grandpa—no matter how much I might like his grumpy self."

"I knew that, but it's nice of you to say it." Her hands moved to his shoulders. "Do you want to hang out for a bit, maybe we can watch a movie or something?"

He kept his hands at her waist as he glanced at the dark TV and the couch. "Tempting, but I need to take a rain check. I have to talk to Rachel—before she leaves for the night shift—about a pretty big favor."

"Oh?" Steph's brows rose. "What's that?"

"Well . . ." He paused. "Maybe we should sit down for a minute."

"Okay . . ." She sat on the couch, and he joined her.

"I was going to wait to tell you until after I talked to Rachel, but I'm thinking of leaving private investigating, and going back to my roots."

Steph's eyes widened. "You mean the renovation stuff you talked about?"

"Exactly," Cal said, his pulse thrumming. She seemed surprised, but not opposed . . . "Despite what happened with my dad, and how everything fell apart, working with Pops on things reminded me of how much I love to build and create. Private investigating keeps me away too much, and I don't want to be out of town when I can do something else I love and be closer to home."

Steph's brows tugged together. "Do you have leads already in Grandin?"

"No . . . I have leads here," he said in a soft voice. "I put in a few calls to references Pops gave me. There's plenty of opportunity in Everly Falls with the older homes that are being bought and sold. Small job upgrades are harder for a larger construction company to take time to do, so I'll fill that niche."

"And move to Everly Falls?" Steph asked, the hope plain in her voice.

"Yes—if you think it's a good idea."

"Why would you need *my* approval?"

Cal held her gaze. "Because there's no reason for me to live here if you didn't want me here."

Steph's smile was slow. "Well, you have my full support. Now come over here and kiss me."

She wasn't very far, and it didn't take much effort to tug her close and kiss her. Steph's curves pressed against him, and her warmth surrounded him. His mind started turning hazy, so it was probably good that Pops called out, "Can someone bring me a drink of water? My feet are done for," or else Cal might have missed talking to Rachel before the night shift after all.

Steph slowly extracted herself from him, a coy smile on her face. "I'm being summoned."

"You are . . . I should get going, though." He rose from the couch and pulled her along with him.

She stepped into his arms, and he drew her close, just breathing her in for a moment.

"Is anyone there?" Pops called out.

"Coming!" Steph smirked. "Don't be a stranger," she whispered, and kissed him once more.

That wouldn't be a problem.

After Cal reluctantly released her, he headed out of the house, pulling the door firmly behind him. His step felt lighter than it had in weeks, probably years. The autumn night air was crisp but not too cold. He inhaled the scent of leaves and let the coolness wash over him. His mind buzzed with plans . . . He hoped to get Rachel's agreement, but if not, he'd find another living situation.

After climbing into his car, excitement pulsed through him as he drove through the neighborhoods of Everly Falls—a place soon to be his home.

Epilogue

One Month Later

STEPH LOOKED IN THE MIRROR, trying to see what Cal might see when he picked her up. She wore a dark red dress, black boots, and she'd done her hair in a loose chignon. Something he might tug out later. She smiled to herself, letting warmth buzz through her. Some days, she wondered if Cal was too good to be true, or if her life was too good to be true. No, nothing was perfect, but it felt pretty near perfect.

She still had to talk herself out of her old thought patterns of not allowing herself to just be, to just enjoy, to just be grateful. Cal was hers, and he was here to stay. No, it wasn't like they were engaged or anything, but she'd never felt so permanent with another person before.

And she was determined to enjoy the evening with her boyfriend.

"Boyfriend," she said to the mirror. "I officially have a boyfriend."

It sounded cheesy when she said it aloud, but the phrase sent goose bumps skittering across her skin. "I officially have a boyfriend, and I think I love him."

She paused, and watched as her skin flushed. Did she love him? The color of her skin was saying yes, but she didn't need it to tell her what she felt. Telling *him* was a different story, of course, but maybe that would happen someday.

Steph released a sigh. She'd be late if she didn't get going on fixing Pops dinner. Yeah, it might be her birthday, but she wasn't going to leave her grandpa hanging. Maybe she could bring him some dessert from whatever restaurant Cal planned to take her to. He told her it was a surprise, so she'd asked, "What should I wear? A dress?"

"Don't you always wear a dress?" he'd replied.

Okay, so he had a fair point.

Her phone buzzed with the ongoing group text. Most of the messages today had been about her birthday.

Have so much fun on your date, Brandy's text read. *Tell us everything!*

I will, Steph wrote.

Yeah, have a blast, Everly texted.

Maren wants a full report of all your birthday presents, Julie added.

Me too, Lori texted.

Steph laughed. *Everyone will get a full report—well, mostly full. If there's kissing, then you'll have to imagine that report.*

Before she closed her phone, an email came through. She opened it and scanned through the message from her new English teacher. She'd signed up for an online English class that she decided would be fun to take. She'd see where things went. Apparently, her teacher had already assigned reading homework. That, she could do. She closed down the email, then slipped her phone into her dress pocket.

Heading out of her bedroom and down the hall, she found Pops sitting in his recliner, with the TV on low and a

Just Add Friendship

crossword in his lap. Cal had told him something about avoiding dementia by doing word puzzles. And Pops pretty much listened to everything Cal said. Tonight, Lydia and Jorge would be coming over for another board game battle with Pops—which meant Steph wouldn't have to worry about him while out with Cal.

When she suggested that she'd be fine if Pops came along, Cal had said that wasn't an option.

"What's for dinner?" Pops asked, without looking up from his crossword.

"How about warmed-up casserole from last night?"

"Sounds perfect."

Cal had actually cooked last night—a giant chicken casserole—and Pops would love the leftovers.

She scooped up a dish, then set it in the microwave. Pops could do all of this, but it was the gesture that Steph thought important. Besides, she was doing much less for her grandpa over the past month than ever. With Cal recently moved to Everly Falls, so many things had changed—for the better.

Cal had set up a collaborative business with Austin and Ian, with them sharing their networks, and even working together at times—Austin with his architecture business, Ian with his handcrafted furniture, and Cal taking on private residence renovations.

He'd told her he was going to start on Pops's house in the spring, but he'd already whipped out a couple of projects—replacing the shelves in the laundry room and adding a small deck that extended from the back door. Pops had been delighted and helped every step of the way.

The microwave dinged. "Pops, dinner is ready," Steph called out.

"I'm right here," he said.

She spun to see him sitting at the kitchen table, a coy smile on his face. "Lost in thought?"

"Apparently," she said, her skin warming.

"Thinking about your man?"

Steph smirked. "Can't share those thoughts."

"You mean you can't kiss and tell?" Pops said.

Where was all this coming from? Oh yeah, Pops was a nosy rooster.

She set the bowl of casserole in front of him, then poured him a glass of milk. Next, she sliced a peach for him. "Do you want toast or anything else?"

"This is excellent," Pops said between bites. "Hitting the spot already."

He was so chipper tonight that it made Steph more grateful for those who were making a difference in his life. It was like he was a new man, and twenty years younger.

When a knock sounded on the door, Pops waved her away. "Stop hovering and let your man inside."

"Yes, sir." She laughed and headed to the door. When she opened it, she stared.

Cal wore a suit and was holding a bouquet of red roses. He was newly shaved, and he was smiling at her. "Happy birthday, Bee."

Should she change into a nicer dress? Cal looked like a million dollars—not that it was hard for him to do—and she could only guess they probably weren't eating at a restaurant in their small town.

"Well, aren't you going to let your boyfriend in the house?" Pops said, sounding a lot closer than the kitchen. "Don't keep him stranded on the porch."

Cal's smile only widened.

"Bye, Pops," she said without looking behind her. She grabbed her purse that she'd put by the door and stepped out onto the porch, pulling the door closed behind her.

Just Add Friendship

"Don't you want to put these in water?"

"No." Steph took the roses and inhaled the sweet fragrance. Then she wrapped her arms around his waist. "Thank you," she murmured. "Best birthday present ever."

"What?" Cal said with a chuckle. "Flowers?"

"Yep."

She could feel his confusion, and she should probably explain, but embracing him and breathing in his aftershave was kind of heaven right now. After a moment, she drew away, but only because Lydia's SUV pulled into their driveway.

"Looks like Pops's company is here," she said. "His social life is really on the upswing."

Cal chuckled and released her. She held his hand, while she carried the roses in the other.

Lydia and Jorge climbed out of the car. "Happy birthday, Stephenie," she said.

"Yeah, happy birthday," Jorge added.

"Thank you." Steph smiled. "Have a nice night with Pops."

"Oh, we will," Lydia said brightly.

Everyone was so happy and chipper, which only made Steph happy herself. *And* it was her birthday, and she'd be with Cal.

"Where are we going?" she asked after they settled into his new truck. Well, it wasn't *new,* but a good condition used truck. Cal said he needed it for his renovations business..

"It's a surprise," he said, flashing her a smile.

"You already told me that." She clutched the roses in her lap and enjoyed the scent filling the cab of the truck. "But now that we're actually on our way, can't you tell me? Or give me a hint?"

Cal turned out of the neighborhood, passing a house on

the corner that had gone all out with its Halloween decorations. "Well, it's someplace you've never been before."

Steph couldn't think of a place she hadn't been before in Everly Falls. "How long's the drive?"

"Only a few minutes."

"That doesn't make sense because if it's in Everly Falls, then I've been there."

Apparently Cal was done giving her hints. "Tell me why you said flowers are your nicest birthday gift."

"Oh . . ." Steph paused. "My parents weren't really into celebrating birthdays. They didn't like following all the holidays and prescribed celebrations. Plus, they said they'd rather spend money on things I needed when I needed them. Not on frivolous things." She shrugged, feeling Cal's gaze on her as they stopped at a traffic light. "As a kid, I felt sorry for myself, but as an adult, I understand more."

"What about holidays?"

"Oh, we celebrated the main ones like Christmas and Thanksgiving, but no presents at Christmas." She released a breath, remembering the shock of learning how her friends were given multiple gifts. "We did a lot of Christmasy things, just not the presents. Pops, of course, thought that was ridiculous and would give me a present. Sweet of him."

Which might have been another clashing point between her mother and Pops.

About ten minutes later, Cal turned into an apartment complex that had a newer development going up on its rear lot. When he parked in front of the new building, she said, "Do you have a friend who lives here?"

"No, I just signed a lease. I'm not moved in yet, but I decided that I like my autonomy too much to live with my aunt again."

"Was she disappointed?"

"Not really."

Steph laughed. "Okay, so we're checking out your empty apartment, then going to eat?"

"No, I have food here."

She was surprised at this. "Already?"

Cal popped open the door, then walked around the truck and helped her out. "You're asking a lot of questions for something that's supposed to be a surprise."

"I'm surprised, and now I want to know more, like why are you wearing a suit?"

He pulled her close and kissed her, which was effective in stopping the questions. For a few minutes. "Come on, Bee."

Maybe he'd set up a card table and a candlelight dinner in the middle of his empty living room?

Cal led her by the hand around a dumpster full of construction refuse. They walked through a short hallway, then stopped at a door.

"You got the ground level—that's nice."

"Yep." He flashed her a grin, then opened the door.

Steph was about to ask why it was unlocked, but the light suddenly turned on, and a chorus of people yelled, "Happy birthday!"

Her heart jolted, and she stared at the gathering of people, taking a second to comprehend. Cal's apartment wasn't empty. It was full of people, and they were singing "Happy Birthday" to her. Steph blinked, then blinked again at the tears burning in her eyes. Her heart was pounding, swelling, her stomach zooming, and she felt like laughing and crying at the same time.

Pops and Lydia and Jorge were front and center. How did they get here so fast? Ian and Brandy, and Everly and Austin with Jessica, and Lori, and Julie and Dave and their kids, and Carol, and all her coworkers from the salon. Cal's aunt Rachel. In the back stood her parents. Her mom's bleached hair was cut into a bob, and she wore a colorful caftan dress. Her father wore a button-down Hawaiian shirt and khakis. Dressed up for both of them.

"Mom?" she mouthed.

Her mother nodded, smile wide. Her father winked at her.

When had they planned to come? How did she not know any of this?

Cal's arm slipped around her, and she leaned against him as the boisterous song wrapped up.

Steph wiped at the tears on her face. "I can't believe this." She looked up at him. "When did you plan this?"

Then she was surrounded by hugs and well-wishes. "How did you get here before me?" she asked Pops.

"Cal drove you the long way."

Once she reached her parents, she hugged them both. "I had no idea you were coming to Everly Falls. When did this all happen?"

"Cal called us a couple of weeks ago," her mom said, adjusting her glasses. "Told us his plans and that it would mean a lot for us to show up."

Steph was speechless. Did Cal pay for their flights? They wouldn't even come out when Pops was in the hospital. "That must have been expensive."

Her parents exchanged glances, then her dad said, "It cost some money, but Cal reminded us that it's been far too long since we visited you. And Pops, of course."

Her mother nodded. "Yes, not that we needed reminding, but it sounded fun to surprise you."

"It's amazing, and I am so surprised." Steph laughed and hugged them again.

When her mother drew back, she said, "Birthdays are important and should be celebrated. We want you to know we're so happy you're our daughter."

More tears came, and Steph swiped them again.

A knock sounded at the door, and someone opened it to a food delivery person bringing sacks of Chinese food. It seemed the restaurant wasn't going to happen after all, but Steph was more than happy to be surrounded by friends and food.

"Were you surprised?" Brandy asked.

"Um, yes!" Steph laughed. "I can't believe Cal got my parents to come. And he wore a suit—completely fooled me."

"I know," Brandy whispered. "And guess what, your parents brought a present."

Steph stared at her friend. "No."

"Yep." She grinned. "I think Cal's good for your family in more ways than one."

"He brought me red roses."

Brandy's brows arched. "Well, you know what that means?"

"That he's a fabulous boyfriend?"

"Yes, but it also means he's going to tell you he loves you."

Steph's face heated. "You can't know that. I mean, it wouldn't be awful, but it's not something you can predict."

Brandy smirked. "It's written all over his face."

Steph snapped her head to look over at Cal, who was talking to Austin and Everly. She turned back to Brandy. "It's not."

She laughed. "It is, and it's written on *your* face."

Steph's first instinct was to deny her comments, even if they were true, but it was nearly impossible to hide things from her best friend. So why bother? "Maybe I'll tell him first," she whispered.

"Ooo, that would be amazing."

"I love your dress," Julie said, joining them. "Now, what are we talking about?"

"We're talking about how cute Maren is holding court over the food." The little girl was currently standing with hands on hips, telling everyone they needed to eat their broccoli in the stir fry.

Julie smirked. "She keeps us on our toes."

"How's the baby?" Steph asked.

"Doing better. Sleeping longer at night."

They all watched Dave with their son for a moment while he talked to Steph's parents.

"I can't believe your parents came out," Julie said. "Did you have any idea?"

"None at all." Steph felt the tears start up again. "I didn't even know Cal had their numbers."

"Probably got them from Pops," Julie suggested.

She nodded. Her gaze skirted the rest of the gathering. Everyone she loved was here—in the same room. It was remarkable. Cal was remarkable.

He looked over at her then, breaking from his conversation with a couple of the men. He'd taken off his suit jacket and loosened his tie. Of course he had. He smiled, and her heart felt like it had expanded. She smiled back, grateful for him and everything about him.

This surprise party was better than anything she could have ever hoped for or imagined.

"Can we open the presents yet?" Maren's little voice cut across a lull in the conversations.

Everyone laughed and looked at Steph.

"Sure, can you help me, Maren?"

"Okay!"

Steph moved to the side of the kitchen counter with a stack of presents. "You all know you didn't have to get me presents."

"Why don't you want presents?" Maren said, her eyes wide.

"Uh, presents are great . . ." She looked to Julie for help, but she just shrugged and smiled. "Can you hand me the first one?"

"Which is the first one?" Maren asked.

"You choose."

For the next few minutes, Steph opened presents, from candles to yummy goodies. Brandy bought her a scarf, and Julie bought her a book she'd been wanting to read that was signed by the author. Lori gave her a gift certificate to a restaurant, and Pops gave her a couple bottles of scented lotion. Her parents gave her a colorful beaded purse from Florida.

When Steph finished, she said, "I feel so spoiled. Thank you so much for coming, everyone." Her gaze connected with Cal's once again. She decided that as great as this party was, she was ready to be with him alone, because she had something to tell him.

It was another hour before the last people left—her parents. They'd refused to stay at Pops's, or at Rachel's, who had also offered, but instead were staying at the bed and breakfast.

"See you tomorrow, then," Steph told them, giving them a final hug before they headed out of Cal's apartment.

When the door shut behind them, Steph turned to see him cleaning up the cartons of food.

He glanced up and paused in what he was doing, a slow smile growing on his handsome face. "Hey."

"Hey." She crossed the room and stepped into his arms. His warm solidness was a place she could stay forever. "Thank you."

"You're welcome," he said in his deep rumble. "Happy birthday, Bee."

She drew back. "I don't know how you pulled it all together. It must have taken you hours."

The edge of his mouth lifted. "Not that long."

She moved her hands across his shoulders.

"Okay, maybe a couple of hours—if I were to add everything up." He scanned her face. "But every second was worth it."

"You know this will be hard to top, don't you?" she said.

His hands moved up her back. "You mean for your next birthday?"

Goose bumps broke out on her skin at his touch. "Yeah—I mean I can't imagine you surprising me again."

"Hmm." His gaze dropped to her mouth. "I guess this means you're keeping me around?"

"If you'll stay around?" she whispered.

"I don't think that's even a question, Bee."

His mouth curved right before he kissed her. She moved her hands to his neck as he pressed her against the counter, taking their kissing very slowly. It was a long moment before he drew away.

"I love you, Steph," he said in a low voice, his gaze holding hers. "I think I have for ten years. I hope that doesn't scare you away."

She only tightened her hold on him. It turned out that Brandy had been right about the roses. "I don't think you could scare me away, because I love you, too. Ten years might be a stretch, though."

He laughed, then pulled her into a tight hug.

She clung to him, her heart drumming, as her stomach did a free-for-all dive. Loving this man had been so easy, she wished she would have allowed herself to fall earlier, much earlier. But he was here now, and she wasn't letting him go.

Heather B. Moore is a *USA Today* bestselling author of more than ninety publications. Heather writes primarily historical and #herstory fiction about the humanity and heroism of the everyday person. Publishing in a breadth of genres, Heather dives into the hearts and souls of her characters, meshing her love of research with her love of storytelling.

Her historicals and thrillers are written under pen name H.B. Moore. She writes women's fiction, romance, and inspirational non-fiction under Heather B. Moore, and . . . speculative fiction under Jane Redd. This can all be confusing, so her kids just call her Mom. Heather attended Cairo American College in Egypt and the Anglican School of Jerusalem in Israel. Despite failing her high school AP English exam, Heather persevered and earned a Bachelor of Science degree from Brigham Young University in something other than English.

For book updates, sign up for Heather's email list:
hbmoore.com/contact

Website: HBMoore.com
Instagram: @authorhbmoore
Facebook: Fans of Heather B. Moore
Blog: MyWritersLair.blogspot.com
Pinterest: HeatherBMoore
TikTok: https://www.tiktok.com/@heatherbmooreauthor
X: @HeatherBMoore

www.ingramcontent.com/pod-product-compliance
Lightning Source LLC
LaVergne TN
LVHW010202070526
838199LV00062B/4465